BULLETS
FOR THE DOCTOR

BULLETS
FOR THE
DOCTOR

Wade Everett

CENTER POINT LARGE PRINT
THORNDIKE, MAINE

This Center Point Large Print edition
is published in the year 2014 by arrangement with
Golden West Literary Agency.

The text of this Large Print edition is unabridged.
In other aspects, this book may vary
from the original edition.

Set in 16-point Times New Roman type.

ISBN: 978-1-62899-316-5

Library of Congress Cataloging-in-Publication Data

Everett, Wade.
Bullets for the Doctor / Wade Everett.
pages cm
Summary: "Two doctors give up the opportunities for safe positions in
the East to set up a practice in Texas where the need for them is greatest
in the post-Civil War era"—Provided by publisher.
ISBN 978-1-62899-316-5 (library binding : alk. paper)
1. Physicians—Fiction. 2. Texas—Fiction. 3. Western stories.
4. Large type books. I. Title.
PS3553.O5547B
813'.54—dc23
2014021445

Printed and bo
by TJ Internati

—1

When I sat down to write about Walter Judson Ivy, I realized instantly that it just wouldn't do to catch up the story at the point where I met him. There was too much to the man for that and too much had gone on before to firm the mold.

He was from a good Baltimore family; his father had been in the manufacturing business, and was certainly well off financially. Young Ivy had been sent to the best private schools where he was taught what a young gentleman was required to learn and he learned it well; indifferent students are not tolerated, either by the parents or the school.

At the age of fourteen, Walter Judson Ivy shocked his parents by running away from home and signing on a vessel bound for the China trade. He returned four years later, taller, heavier, quite sober and he had an enormous tattoo on his right forearm, which caused his mother to swoon and his father to swear profoundly, and then cast him out of the house.

All of which bothered Walter J. Ivy not at all.

He surprised his father by enrolling in a medical school, paying for it out of his own pocket from savings. His graduation three years later so stirred the pride of Ivy's parents that the Baltimore home was now open to him.

But fathers are always making plans for their sons and sons are always disappointing their fathers; it seems a role each is destined to play. Walter Ivy's father expected him to take up residency in one of the Baltimore hospitals, but young Ivy had a cantankerous streak in him and hied off to Texas. He set up practice in Goliad, which so incensed Ivy senior that he wouldn't even look up the location in his atlas.

And Walter Ivy fanned these fires of disappointment by sending home newspaper accounts of Goliad's wild and lawless development. Ivy's office was a two-room affair over the bank and he set broken bones and delivered babies and plucked cap-and-ball lead out of various and sundry lawless persons who could not seem to keep out of trouble.

Texas, in 1858, was not a land of tranquility.

Walter J. Ivy was twenty-five when the War between the States broke out and he returned east immediately and took a commission as captain in the medical department. He served tirelessly and well and emerged a lieutenant-colonel, which of course softened his father's heart and the Baltimore home was again open.

A man of commanding presence, Walter J. Ivy was tall and strongly built, with a high forehead and rather thin, tawny hair. He had dense eyebrows and the habit, when vexed or troubled, of shooting them upward so that they seemed in danger of colliding with his hair. His eyes were rather gray with flecks of gold in them and his manner of steadily watching a person could be disconcerting, especially if one was bothered by a feeling of guilt or inadequacy. He always wore a mustache, but kept it trimmed as a concession to hygiene more than to style.

The war's end was many things to many men. To Walter Ivy it was a tiring horror and he was glad to be rid of it, but to his father, who had grown wealthy manufacturing needed goods, it was the termination of large profits. This is not to say that he was a heartless man who enjoyed war; he loathed it and prayed for a quick end to it, yet he was a business man who could not ignore the profit of it.

Walter J. Ivy was twenty-nine years old when he returned to Baltimore, and in his father's conservative mind, this was time to enter the institution of marriage and he went about the business of finding a suitable wife.

As Walter tells it, parties and dances and teas and social affairs were arranged so that he was flung headlong into this cultural pit of dry-mannered, predatory females who batted their eyes and promised pleasures and comforts after the church bells stopped pealing and finally he had a craw full and packed up and left, neglecting, as usual, to announce his intentions.

The world was turning and Walter Ivy felt that he was being left out and the next word his parents received of his whereabouts was a postcard from Fort Reno; Ivy had returned to the army and the Indian campaigns were getting under way and he was simply a man who couldn't miss any of it.

Two years later, in 1867, he was at Fort Grant, Arizona Territory, a post reactivated to do battle with the war-like Apaches, and here I enter, Ted Bodry, nineteen years and two months, a corpsman in the medical department and attached to Colonel Ivy's staff.

I was one of those who resented being born too late for the war and as soon as I finished high school, I enlisted. At nineteen one has few choices and I rejected being a bugler because I have a poor ear for music, so I took what was left, the medical department.

It is hard to say what attracted Colonel Ivy's attention to me; I would like to flatter myself and think that it was because I tried very hard to do my duty well. Whatever it was, I became his orderly and this was the pivotal point in my life.

It was Walter Ivy's urging that led me to accept an early discharge, and it was Walter Ivy who put me on the eastbound stage and it was Walter Ivy who handed me my letter of introduction and recommendation to the dean of the medical school.

I didn't see him again until 1869 when he came home on leave. He was very pale and drawn and he carried a heavy cane and walked with a pronounced limp. Knowing him, it was needless for me to ask how he had been wounded, for he was a selfless man who often risked much to help someone.

I first knew he was back when I was summoned to the dean's office; Walter Ivy sat in a big leather chair by the dean's desk and he got up when I came in and we shook hands. He looked at me, noted the changes two years had made, then smiled and waved his hand for me to sit down.

"I've been looking at your scholastic record, Ted. It seems that one day you'll be a doctor."

"Yes, sir. Next year."

"I'll be in the east for a year," he said, "and I'd take it kindly if you'd spend the holidays with me. Perhaps I could drop in on you from time to time."

"I'd be very flattered, sir."

"Good," he said, feeling that the matter was settled. He smiled and got up slowly and offered his hand again. "I don't want to keep you from your classes, Ted. And I must get home and gird myself to resist the attempts being made to see me married. Father believes that a woman makes a lamb of any man."

I saw him three times after that, then the wild goose called and in 1870 he returned west, to

Camp Apache, Arizona Territory and he remained there nearly a year.

My term of study was finished with surprisingly high marks. Graduation approached and all along I expected a letter from Walter Ivy, offering his congratulations, or something.

But there wasn't anything, and this struck me as odd because I knew he had paid my tuition for three years.

I sat on the platform with my graduating class and looked at the sea of faces and wished that my own parents had lived to see this, then I caught a movement in the back of the hall and Walter J. Ivy walked down the aisle and took a seat near the front. He looked at me and smiled and put everything right with me.

Afterward we went for a walk, Theodore Bodry, M.D. and Walter J. Ivy, M.D. and we fed the birds in the park and watched the swans in the lake and listened to some young fellow serenade his girl with a banjo and an unstable tenor. We could hear her squeals of delighted terror as he rocked the boat, then he would play and she would say, "Oh, Herman, you play divinely." Which he didn't, but then love can make a masterpiece of any tawdry canvas.

We talked about what I would do and I expressed a desire to remain in the east for perhaps a year and intern at some hospital to gain surgical experience. Even as I said it, I knew that I had disappointed him and I was sorry to do that, but I kept repeating that I felt unqualified to establish a practice alone.

The position I finally got was in a small overworked charity hospital and the pay was only two dollars a week, with long hours, poor meals, and a small room of my own.

Walter Ivy and I did not see each other for four months, but I knew that he was still in Baltimore. He was being seen everywhere with Dorsey Pribble, the only daughter of *the* Pribbles, who everyone figured were about as high as you could go with money and good blood.

She was a beauty of the first water, in her early twenties, an intensely courted young woman who had yet to find a man who suited her. Yet she found Walter Ivy attractive enough and there was little doubt in anyone's mind that Ivy had at last fallen in love. But if he had, it wasn't enough to keep him home.

Leaving the army, he went to Victoria, Texas, and established a practice there; I learned this when he wrote and asked me to join him and it took me two hours to pack my bags, buy my ticket and board the westbound train.

Of course this upset Ivy's family and Ivy senior was furious. Mr. and Mrs. Pribble forbade Dorsey ever to speak his name, and when Walter Ivy wrote her, the loyal maid promptly gave the letter to Mr. Pribble, who threw it in the fireplace.

Mr. Pribble believed it was his duty to shield his

daughter from cads and irresponsible bounders.

Several letters followed the first into the fire and I arrived in Victoria just in time to take over Walter's practice while he carried out some important private business.

He appeared suddenly at the Pribble house and had some violent words with Mr. Pribble, who just wasn't used to being talked to that way. Mrs. Pribble went into a swoon over the whole affair, which didn't last long because Walter left on the two o'clock train.

Taking Dorsey Pribble with him, of course.

They were married when the train stopped to take on fuel and additional coaches and in the years that followed I always wondered if he went back because he realized that he could not live without her or whether she came west with him because she knew he'd never come back east to stay.

I would say that the entire town turned out to greet them when they got off the stage coach. (In 1873 the trains did not probe that far south and every traveler had to ride the stages.)

Victoria in 1873 was the kind of town that took on a completely different complexion on Saturday night, when everyone for miles around came in to shop and talk and play cards and drink and see the professional girls who kept houses in the back of the main street. Quarrels that began on the range over water or graze were settled in Victoria, and no Saturday evenings ever passed without the sound of pistol fire. And now and then the bullets were directed at objects other than the moon. Curiosity drew a crowd to Pringer's Hotel, where the stage line kept a passenger office. Walter Ivy was a popular man and it was only good manners to pay respects to the new bride. I was on a call at the time and couldn't be there, but Aaron Stiles ran a vivid account of it in his paper. She was, according to Stiles, beautiful, young, and a bit alarmed but she had breeding and pride and seemed to accept the hooraw with friendliness. For Victoria, Texas, of the quick-trigger, quick-judgment school, this was more than enough and to all appearances, at least according to Stiles's fulsome article, the town had instantly accepted Dorsey Ivy.

Long before Walter Ivy went east to claim his bride, he had begun construction of a house and offices at the west edge of town. He selected a shady spot and the house was still full of sawed pine and paint flavors when he carried the lady across the threshold. Furniture had been wagoned in from Austin, the terminus of the railroad in those days, and a deep carpet covered the parlor floor and drapes hung heavy over the windows.

His offices were in the east wing of the house, five rooms, one serving as a five-bed hospital. I shared these offices with Walter Ivy and the night he got home it was well after dark when I put my

15

horse in the barn and walked toward the house, not realizing until I reached the porch that he was back.

The housekeeper let me in, took my bag and coat and pistol—any man, even a doctor, would indeed be foolish to travel without a firearm with Indians about—then she said, "Dr. Ivy has returned with his bride."

"Well I'll be go to the devil," I said.

He must have heard me, heard our voices; anyway he came to stand in the kitchen doorway. "Ted," he said, laughing. "Come in here now."

When I came up to him he took my arm and steered me into the kitchen. "Dorsey, this is Dr. Ted Bodry, whom I've spoken of so often."

She turned from the stove where she had been making coffee and she looked directly at me with the brownest eyes I have ever seen. In my opinion she was taller than average; I would judge near five-foot-eight, but she had a magnificent figure. Her face was inclined to the square side, but well-proportioned, with fine bones and a good jaw.

When she took my hand I was surprised to find it warm; most women have cold hands. I liked her, and perhaps I was instantly on guard against her, if you can understand how it can be proper to feel so about another man's wife. "Ted, I really have heard much about you. Walter is very proud of you."

But she looked at my youth and inexperience

and rather made me feel as though I should apologize for it. I let go of her hand and said, "I won't ask you how you like Texas because most people who come here don't. But I can promise that it has a certain charm although I haven't yet discovered what it is."

"I'm sure I will," she said. "Women are very adaptable. Would you like some coffee?"

"Did you make it or did Mrs. Hempstead?"

"Why, I did." She laughed. "Does it matter?"

"After you drink it awhile, it does," Walter said and sat down at the table. She brought cups and sugar and cream. I rubbed my eyes because I'd been on the go since a quarter to six that morning. Walter said, "Did Mrs. Lovering come to her time?"

"Delivered day before yesterday. A girl. Everything is fine. I took a shoat and six layers. Is that all right?"

Dorsey frowned. "Shoat? Isn't that a pig?"

"A pig it is. And six laying hens. I'd say we were well paid, Doctor." He lifted his wife's hand and kissed it. "My dear, sometimes we even get money for our services. Isn't that right, Ted?"

"Yes," I agreed. I glanced at Dorsey, then said, "I picked up a new patient while you were gone. One of Dirty Esther's girls came to me with symptoms that I diagnosed as gonorrheal urethritis. Naturally it's advanced, as you'd expect it to be. Chronic bilateral salpingitis."

17

Dorsey touched Walter Ivy on the arm. "Is he talking about what I think he's talking about? At the table? In mixed company?"

"Yes, he's talking about a woman of easy virtue who has a social disease," Walter Ivy said. "Not a delicate subject, my dear, but,"—and he sighed over this—"we treat the sick without judging them, or asking for credentials."

"The poor woman," Dorsey said, genuinely touched. She reached out and patted my arm. "You go right ahead and discuss your cases, Ted. I will simply have to learn to be a doctor's wife. And I will."

And she did, but it took a long time.

—2

That summer stands out in my mind, not because it was a particularly good summer, but because it was an eventful one. The two biggest cow outfits were the Spindle and the T-Cross; they each carried a hundred men on the payroll and since they both made cattle drives north each spring, they both had money and a lot of it.

Of the two outfits, Spindle was a little better situated; they had the best water because Old Man Brittles got his crew to dam up some reservoirs. This cost him a good bit of money and

Beachamp of the T-Cross thought it was a great foolishness and a waste. And a lot of people sided with Beachamp because he'd been there ten years and the summers were blessed with thunder showers which kept the creeks up and the grass green.

But that summer the last rain came on the seventeenth of April, and it wasn't much of a rain, lasting barely the afternoon. Of course, at the time none of us knew it was going to be the last rain and as a matter of fact no one paid any attention to it, except me.

An emergency call to a small ranch eight miles out of town got me out of bed around dawn; the father was highly agitated so when I went out to hitch up the buckboard, I took a look at the cloudless sky and left town with nothing more than my medical bag, a shotgun and a rolled raincoat.

Walter Ivy had delivered the Stiles' baby four days before and at the time I was in the northern part of the county officiating as coroner. (Walter and I had agreed to rotate this civic duty on a yearly basis.) So the Stiles' baby was really Walter Ivy's patient, but he was in Austin trying to increase his usual purchase of medical supplies and I was on my way to Pete Stiles' place.

Because we hurried, we made the distance in a shade under two hours and I went in to see what I could do. Stiles was a poor man, twenty-some, a hard worker trying to make a go on one section. His wife was young, about fifteen, and this was her first child.

They lived in one big room and she was holding the baby when I came in. Stiles stood awkwardly as fathers do when they are helpless and I put down my hat, shotgun and bag and asked a few questions.

"What seems to be wrong?"

"He pukes all the time," Mrs. Stiles said.

I took the baby from her and laid him on the table and examined him. He was obviously not gaining weight and he had thin, dry, loose skin. It was apparent that he was getting little nourishment and I turned to ask her if her breasts were drying up, but the question was needless. She was swollen and in discomfort and the front of her dress was damp from leakage.

After examining the infant's eyes, I listened to his heart, thumped him front and back, then said, "Mrs. Stiles, will you please nurse the child?"

Already I was reaching a conclusion, but I wanted to make sure.

Stiles started to make a fuss about, "My wife ain't goin' to show her tits—"

I ran him out of the house.

Mrs. Stiles nursed the baby for a moment or two; he was very weak and could barely nurse, then he was seized with a fit of projectile vomiting.

"I'll have to take the baby into town," I said and went to the door to call Stiles. He came in and stood there, not knowing what to do. "The child has pyloric stenosis." He didn't understand and to keep it from sounding dreadful, I tried to explain what the matter was all about. "This is a spasm of the pyloris muscle which acts as a valve and closes off the discharge end of the stomach. However I believe this is congenital. That is, I believe he was born with a restriction."

"Is he goin' to die?" Stiles asked.

"I'll have to perform an operation. Usually it is quite simple and safe. That's why I want you to put some straw in the back of the buckboard and ride into town with me."

He jawed and argued and didn't want his child cut into and cut up a fuss, but there's no need to go into that because I won out and took the child to town. And it rained on the way and because Stiles owned no slicker, we wrapped the baby in mine, and I got soaked to the skin.

I operated that afternoon and the child showed immediate signs of recovery while I showed signs of coming down with a good cold. The child returned home in three days and Walter Ivy came back in time to let me go to bed with a roaring fever.

In his absence I had made nearly thirty house calls, plucked two bullets out of the stage driver after a brief brush with Comanches, delivered the

Wringle baby which came ten days earlier than either of us expected—but you run into those things when a wife insists on plowing in that condition—and performed the abdominal surgery on the Stiles' infant, for which I had collected the sum of nineteen dollars, some poultry, a calf, a gold watch which I was holding in trust, and many words of thanks.

Over the years I've clung to the firm belief that few, if any, modern doctors can comprehend the demands made on a physician and surgeon in frontier practice. San Antonio, nearly a hundred miles to the northwest, boasted three doctors, and Goliad, a little more than half that distance to the southwest, had one doctor, for Walter Ivy had once practiced there and he never left a town unless he could get a doctor and a druggist to establish themselves there.

Still we served an immense country, three counties really and often we would ride for two days to tend a person too ill to be brought to us. It was a dangerous time with the Indians and all, and all men, save perhaps the boy boxing groceries in the store, performed dangerous work. And even that was not without risk because Linus Cohill's horse kicked him one afternoon, broke three ribs, then dragged the iron-shod rim of the wagon wheel over his foot and broke two toes.

Add to this the firearms-supported arguments, the broken bones from horse wrangling and the gorings from wild Texas cattle and it added up to a lively practice because all these things were in addition to the child bearing and the fevers and diseases which plague the innocent.

Since Walter Ivy and myself were considered well educated, we had other responsibilities. As I mentioned, we took turns being county coroner. This was not an attempt to evade responsibility, but since we served two counties, I was coroner in one while Walter Ivy served the other. Each year we swapped, running unopposed, and I suppose, being elected unanimously. At least I never talked to a man who had voted against us.

Walter was a Free Mason and was one of the Worthy-something-or-other; I was an Odd Fellow myself and pretty deeply entrenched in that. I'll never understand how I got on the school board and town council, and Walter to this day swears that his being a deacon in the Baptist Church was an accident since he had been an Episcopalian all his life.

So I was in bed with a fever when Walter got back from Austin and Dorsey was nursing me and all day long bringing in a steady stream of people who wanted to know what "Causes this terrible pain in my back, Doctor?"

Yes, that was the summer all right, with a scalding sun and heat like a blanket every day. It was a summer exactly suited to a young man when the juices ran strong and he could go to bed exhausted and wake up with a bounce.

That was the summer when everyone watched the sky for the rain that never came and finally, around August, the creeks were down to a trickle and Beachamp started looking hate at those watersheds on Spindle land and watching Spindle steers fatten, for Brittles was going to weather it out and Beachamp knew that he couldn't.

I don't think there was anyone who didn't know that trouble was coming, but none of us knew what to do to head it off. Now and then, when we were lucky enough to get to sit down to a meal together we'd talk about it. Tempers, especially between the two spreads, were growing wire tight, and to keep things from coming to a head, Brittles had taken to bringing his crew in on Friday night and leaving the town to T-Cross on Saturday.

We all hoped that this would work and complimented Brittles on his consideration; the old man had fought for his land and knew what range war meant. Brittles knew that there was nothing wrong that a good rain wouldn't cure.

But come September it hadn't rained a drop.

There weren't even any clouds in the sky.

I was in my office at mid-afternoon, trying to rest because I had a patient eleven miles out of town who would be starting labor any time and since it was her first child, I was a bit concerned that it would take some time.

Dorsey knocked on my door, which was odd because she didn't do that unless I had a patient, and she knew that I was alone. She wore a thin cotton dress, trying to defend herself against the heat, but sweat darkened the shoulders and ran in small rivulets down her neck.

She sat down and said, "Dr. Bodry, I'd like to discuss pregnancy."

This brought my eyes open and she laughed softly. "Does Walter—"

"I don't think doctors like to attend their wives unless they have to," she said. "I've missed two periods."

We discussed the situation briefly and an examination confirmed her suspicions. I placed the birth somewhere in the middle of April and she seemed very pleased with herself. "He'll be wonderful with children," she said. "Of course, I'll have to write mother. Perhaps this—"

It wasn't my place to pry, but we were good friends, so I asked, "Dorsey, are you happy here?"

"Yes, Ted, happier than I've ever been."

"But you'd be happier if your mother would answer your letters," I said. "It's a rotten shame, that's what it is! People have to understand."

"It takes time," she said and got up from her chair. "Walter will be home tonight. While you're at lodge I'll tell him."

"You're young and strong and have good

bones," I said, "and there are no reasons for concern or complications."

"I'm not afraid, Ted."

"Well, no, I didn't mean that," I said. "If Walter begins to act like a typical father—"

She shook her head. "Walter has never been a typical anything. It's part of his charm." Then she smiled again and went out and I was very pleased; Walter Ivy deserved a child and I hoped that it would be a boy.

Since it was my lodge night, I ate at the hotel, played a few games of pool, bought several cigars and walked three blocks east to the Odd Fellows hall. Afterward I had a drink at the bar, talked about the heat and the damned rain that kept holding off, then went home.

Since Walter had returned with his wife, I used a small side room behind my office for sleeping quarters; it was ample for a bachelor and my comings and goings would not disturb them in the least.

I intended to travel at night to avoid the heat and I was in the barn, hitching up the buckboard when Walter Ivy came out. He leaned against a post for a moment, then said, "Ted, when you examined Dorsey, did you notice anything that—"

"She's very healthy," I said, "and I predict a normal delivery. Didn't she tell you that?"

"Yes, but I thought she was setting my mind at ease." He rubbed the back of his neck. "You have no idea how this pleases me, Ted, but we must take care. Nothing must happen to her."

"Nothing will, Walter."

"Yes, yes, I'm sure, still I wish you'd examine urine specimens frequently. If there's any toxemia or a possible diabetes mellitus—" He pawed his mouth out of shape and busied himself with the lighting of a cigar. "Pyelitis takes so many woman in childbirth that—"

"Walter, you know I'll take every precaution," I said. "And Dorsey said you wouldn't act like a typical father."

"Did she say that?" He smiled. "Well, I'm not typical. I'm a doctor and can keep my worry specific."

"Keep this up and you'll turn into an old fud," I said and checked my shotgun before getting into the buggy. Then I made sure my bag was complete, got in and backed out of the barn.

"When can I expect you back?" Walter asked.

I counted the days in my mind. "Try Saturday late, if the Indians don't get me."

"That's not very funny. You have your pistol?"

"Put it on with my pants," I said and drove out of the yard, taking the south road toward the Espirito Santo Mission, ruins now, but a landmark still.

Night traveling had the advantage of minimizing worry about the Indians for they were governed largely by superstition and would not sally forth at night. Still it was no time for a man to doze and I drove with the shotgun across my knee, keeping to a pace that would cover miles and yet save the team.

I cut across T-Cross land and after midnight I raised a line shack.

Three men melted out of the darkness, all heavily armed and I identified myself. Then a lamp was lighted and someone stirred up the fire and put on coffee.

No one thought it strange that I'd be about late at night; a doctor goes all the time, everywhere. I went into the shack and had my coffee, mentioning casually my destination and they nodded, taking note of this; they weren't a gabby bunch at all.

Refreshed, I got into the rig again and rode out, not stopping until the first flush of dawn brightened the sky and pushed back the darkness across the land. My destination was not far, a scant eight or nine miles and I reckoned to make it before the morning heat grew too intense.

The land was quiet. That sounds strange to say, upon reflection, but that was the way it was. Quiet. And land isn't quiet for there are birds hawking and wheeling and animals in the grass rustling about and there is a living, pulsating sound to the land that was now totally absent.

This alerted me and I shifted my pistol holster around to where it was handier and cocked my shotgun and kept one hand on it always. The country was rolling, grassy, with trees dotting the hillsides and I kept an eye on the ridges for there the trouble would come, if it came.

For miles I rode through this vast silence, seeing nothing at all, and then I came to the fork in the road that would lead me to Carl Rowan's place and I followed the path; it was hardly more than that, a bit of grass trampled by the infrequent passage of his wagon.

Finally I could smell smoke. Not fresh smoke, but that strong, rank flavor left by a dead fire and I lashed my team to a quicker pace. Topping a slight rise, I saw the Rowan place, ashes now, with the stone chimney partially crumbled and the fences down and the cattle slaughtered and Rowan, fire-blackened, in the yard where the Comanches had left him.

I knew they would have never taken Mrs. Rowan, not heavy with child, so I got out of the buggy and began to cut a circle around the place until I found her. She was dead, and from the terrible hatchet wound in her head, it had come mercifully quick.

The Indians leave destruction that boggles the mind of man and makes him wonder what possesses them to break every breakable thing they can get their hands on. Rowan's plow was reduced to rubble and I rummaged around what was left of his tool shed and selected a shovel whose handle, although broken, was longer than the others.

I spent the rest of the morning digging graves, and sometimes that was a doctor's duty too.

—**3**

When I returned to town and made my report to the sheriff, it did not cause any alarm; rather it made everyone gloomy, as though with the heat and drought they had to have Indian trouble too. Rowan had some kin over Fort Duncan way and I wrote them a letter, explaining the circumstances, as I knew them, and offered my sympathy and the assurance that they were buried in a Christian manner and that suitable markers had been placed over the graves.

The sheriff and a party of four well-armed men rode out to see if they could pick up the Indians' trail, but I didn't think much would come of that and I expect they didn't either, but they were going to try. Now and then the Indians grew bold and careless and were caught.

A lot of good it did.

Walter Ivy had a case that he thought would be interesting to me and after a lunch at his home, we got into his buggy and drove across town to what was Victoria's better section; the people with the most money seemed to settle there: the banker and the storekeepers and two retired Confederate army officers, if you can consider any Confederate officer "retired." Many thought that Dr. Ivy ought to live in that section, but he wouldn't hear of it and I suppose it was because he had been raised in a proper house on a proper street and naturally rebelled against the idea of conformity.

As we drove along he discussed the case: "Yesterday, I got a call from Butram Cardine at the bank. His son, Lunsford, had been taken ill and he wanted me to look in on him. I went to the home and found the young man in bed. He complained of feeling poorly for over a week now, having a sore throat, general malaise, and a low fever."

"Have you examined a blood sample under the microscope?"

Walter Ivy smiled. "Of course. Do you think I'm one of those backward country doctors? The blood spread shows large numbers of mono-nuclear cells."

"Sounds like virus hepatitis," I said quickly.

"Possibly," Ivy agreed. "But I'd like to have you examine him. I would hate to make a hasty diagnosis of the case and be wrong."

I laughed. "Yes, Cardine is a man of influence."

"To hell with that," Ivy snapped. "I don't like to be wrong with any patient."

We stopped in front of the banker's home; it was a huge white house crouched among huge trees and a colored servant hastened out to take our horses around in back.

A maid opened the front door and we stepped inside. Sunlight through the stained glass foyer windows spread color into the deep green rug. Mrs. Cardine was a rather frail, flighty woman who kept wringing her hands and making puckers with her lips. Lunsford was upstairs, in his room and as we went up the stairs I kept thinking that I didn't like him much. He was near my age and as arrogant as wealth and position could make him, and the damned man was outright handsome, tall and broad through the shoulders; he was everything I wasn't and I know it was childish, but I resented him no end.

The curtains were drawn to protect his eyes and I opened one near his bed to conduct an examination. His complexion was rather jaundiced, which pretty much confirmed my opinion that he had hepatitis. Really, I could have concluded my examination quickly, but I could not resist taking his temperature. Normally an oral temperature will suffice, and I know that Walter, in dealing with sensitive women, became very Continental and took the temperature under the armpit.

This would not satisfy me and I put Lundsford Cardine through the position and took a rectal temperature, and knew when I did it that I was making a lifelong enemy.

He had a good fever all right, which cinched things in my mind.

Walter Ivy looked at his watch and said, "Lunsford, you're going to get better in no time. Didn't I see you at the dance two weeks ago?"

He nodded and Ivy patted his arm in a patronizing manner. "Well, you'll be dancing again soon."

We went out and Ivy remained a moment to offer Mrs. Cardine words of encouragement, and to give her instructions. When he got into the buggy, he said, "What do you think?"

"Virus hepatitis."

"Sure?"

"Yes, I'm sure."

He clucked to the team, turned them and drove down a block and a half and stopped at Rolle Dollar's house. I said, "Is Angeline ill?"

"Feeling poorly," Ivy said and took his bag and we walked to the front door.

Let me say now that I had a special interest in Angeline Dollar; she was eighteen and quite lovely and because her father was very religious, she led an extremely sheltered life, so much so that my desire to call on her socially was constantly being put off by her parents' rigid conformity to manners and morals.

Her mother met us at the door and we went

33

to Angeline's room; it was a dainty place with lace curtains over the windows and a wallpaper designed to reflect the feminine mood.

Angeline was in bed, as I expected her to be and Ivy smiled and sat down and felt her pulse. "You know Dr. Bodry, of course. How are you feeling? I thought I'd bring Dr. Bodry along to examine you. We want to find out just what kind of a bug has bitten you."

"That's nice of you, Dr. Walter," she said and smiled at me with devastating effect. Ivy got up and I sat on the edge of her bed. Examining a woman generally bothered me not at all, but to place my stethoscope against the round bareness of her breast was an experience nigh onto unnerving. When I wiped my thermometer with alcohol and shook it, Walter Ivy watched me carefully, and when I had her tuck it under her armpit, he said, "That's not your accustomed procedure, is it, Doctor?"

I had never been so embarrassed.

And it was difficult to think properly with her blue eyes constantly on me, watching my every expression. She had a fever, not very high, but one of those steady burners that promised to mount dangerously.

Her mother stood by the door, her expression drawn with worry. "Is it serious, Doctor?"

Walter Ivy shook his head. "I really don't think so."

This rather angered me for I had concluded that she had a good virus going and Ivy was making light of it; I consider it an error to delude patients or their families. Still, she was his patient and I held my tongue.

Walter Ivy said, "Angeline, did you go to the dance a few weeks ago?"

"She's not allowed to carry on," Mrs. Dollar snapped. "It was rude of you to ask."

"Of course," Ivy said, mollified. "Do you have any coffee, Mrs. Dollar? A cup would certainly be refreshing. Don't you agree, Doctor?"

"Yes," I said, wondering what he was getting at; he was not a man easily molded by suggestion or force.

"I'll put it on," Mrs. Dollar said and left the room.

When her step faded on the stairs, Ivy looked at Angeline and said, "I know you went to the dance with young Cardine. I'm afraid it'll have to come out, my dear."

The beast made her cry and then he stood there, insensitive to her tears. "Come along, Doctor," he said dryly.

"Really, Walter, this is highly irregular!" Her tears and his manner riled me.

"Try to be clinical, Doctor. She has infectious mononucleosis, commonly called kissing disease. If you read your medical journals more carefully you would have seen my paper on it. It is a virus infection in which the lymph nodes and blood cells are attacked by pathogens." He opened the door to go downstairs. "Dry her eyes if you must but don't kiss her. Not yet at least!"

I thought that last barb totally unwarranted and I patted Angeline's hand, assured her that everything would be all right in spite of this uncouth horse doctor and then followed Ivy to the parlor where Mrs. Dollar was setting out the coffee cups. Walter Ivy was the soul of grace and politeness; he chatted a moment, clearly avoiding the subject of Angeline's illness.

But Mrs. Dollar wouldn't be put off, as I knew she couldn't, and as Walter Ivy knew she wouldn't. "Angeline complained of feeling poorly several days ago but I thought nothing of it."

"A sore throat?" Ivy asked.

"Why—yes."

"And a feeling of uneasiness? Perhaps a suggestion of upset stomach?"

"Why—that's it exactly!"

"And of course the fever and the swollen lymph nodes throughout the body," Ivy said, looking at me. "Do you still think it's—"

I waved my hand and drank my coffee; I'd made a big enough fool of myself and it was another Walter Ivy lesson ground in properly.

"Mrs. Dollar, Angeline is suffering from what we call infectious mononucleosis, commonly called, 'kissing disease.' "

I'm positive anyone down the street heard her gasp in shock and dismay. "DoooocTORIIIvy!" she said. "This is unthinkable!"

"Well, that well may be but this disease generally breaks out into an epidemic following dances and general social events where partners of the opposite sex exchange 'soul kisses.' "

I thought she was going to faint; she sagged into a chair, one hand to her breast, her eyes rolling heavenward and I reached for my bag and the smelling salts but Walter Ivy waved me motionless.

"Now, now, Mrs. Dollar, we mustn't let our narrow little minds run away with us. Your daughter, I'm happy to say, is a young girl with strong natural impulses, and young Cardine suffers from the same illness, only in a more advanced stage. When I first examined him, I was misled as Dr. Bodry was, then I began to suspect that he had picked it up from someone, although not in this community. Then when your husband asked me to look in on—"

"Please! Please spare me the horror of it all!" Mrs. Dollar cried.

"Madam, you're dramatizing this entirely out of proportion," Ivy said flatly. Then he did a thing that shocked me; he took her by both arms and shook her until her head bobbed violently and her eyes rolled. "Now listen carefully to me, madam! Your daughter will recover quite naturally in a week or ten days; I'll have Dr. Bodry check on her daily." He looked at me and there was a twinkle in his eyes. "I'm sure he can find time in his schedule."

"Yes," I said and let it go at that. Mrs. Dollar was staring transfixed at Walter Ivy; she had probably never been spoken to quite like that.

"Now I have a few instructions that you will follow to the letter," Ivy said. "Is that clearly understood?" She nodded meekly. "Personal hygiene is very important with the patient; she will take a tub bath daily and wash her hands after voiding. Each morning, immediately after breakfast, she will evacuate the bowels." Again that shocked gasp, but Ivy went on. "To encourage this, give her two glasses of hot fluid upon awakening. Add one teaspoon of bicarbonate of soda and flavor it with tea or lemon juice. Persuade her to remain up as long as possible and to walk around the porch or sit in front of an open window. Fresh air is important. Do not fuss with her diet; allow her to eat and drink what she pleases, but see that she gets lots of fluids." He released his grip and allowed her to relax in the chair. "I'll write out these instructions so you'll make no mistake. Pull yourself together, Mrs. Dollar. This disease is common enough—"

"Common?" She pressed her knuckles to her mouth, turned her head away and cried.

Ivy motioned for me to go upstairs and I was

eager enough to do that for Angeline was in a bit of trouble and she should be prepared for it. I knocked lightly and went in and sat on the edge of her bed. "I suppose you heard the wailing downstairs? Well, it'll soon blow over and be forgotten." I took her hand and held it. "Do you think it was worth it?"

She knew what I meant and blushed and turned her face away. "You must think I'm terrible."

"I don't think that at all, and I'll be in to see you every day."

Walter Ivy was waiting for me in the buggy and when I got in, he said, "She'll catch the devil for this all right. Well, into each life a little rain must fall."

"Oh, damn your platitudes," I said and sulked a bit, and felt a little frustrated.

Walter Ivy said, "Just can't make up your mind, can you, Ted?"

"About what?"

"What irritates you more, being wrong in your diagnosis or because Lunsford Cardine had the fun of soul kissin—"

"All right, Walter. Never mind!"

That evening, Dorsey insisted that I have supper with them and since I had no house calls until seven-thirty, I accepted the invitation; I tire quickly of hotel meals for the cooking is not always the best and the diet is very limited: beef, beans, potatoes, tomatoes and greens when in season, bad pie and worse coffee. Travelers, pausing briefly in their journey really have no time to complain, but local people like myself, who haven't the time to prepare meals, have to suffer along with the soda bottle handy and indigestion right around the corner.

As a doctor, it is easy for me to spot a patient who is a bachelor and habitué of hotels and Mexican restaurants; they are overweight from greasy foods, suffer chronic indigestion and constipation, and have foul dispositions.

Mrs. Hempstead, the housekeeper, could pan broil a chicken such as you have never tasted and her pot roast was the talk of south Texas long before the Comanches wiped out her family and she came to work for Walter Ivy.

The thought of one of her meals was a delight and I overate, as usual, especially when it came to the peach pie. With my call I had to excuse myself early and Walter agreed to meet me in Sharniki's pool hall for a game around nine o'clock, and I was positive I'd be through by then.

I had two calls, both in town. The blacksmith, in shoeing an ox—and they are devils at best—sustained a fractured arm, and since Walter and I had been toying with the plaster of paris and cloth cast, I wanted to check and see if swelling was binding it anywhere and causing him pain.

Fortunately it was not; we had a beer, talked a bit and I went across town where I had an elderly patient with an unoperable tumor.

So it was about fifteen minutes to nine when I reached the pool hall. A sultry, dense heat lay over the town and the temperature was still in the nineties. To the south, heat lightning split the sky in ragged streaks; it seemed to be almost a nightly occurrence, but it held no promise of rain although they were getting it around Refuge and San Patricio.

The heat and the lightning only made us envious of those who enjoyed the cooling benefits of rain.

Most of Buford Brittles' riders were in town, you could hear them down the street, whooping it up in the saloon and Buford was in the pool hall, playing solitaire. Since Walter Ivy hadn't arrived, I played two hands of double with Brittles; we didn't talk much. Everyone lost their taste for conversation in this heat.

Then Walter Ivy came in and I finished my game and selected a pool cue. He took the break and was pretty decent about it, scattering the balls all over the table. I ran a seven ball in the corner pocket and was lining up the nine ball when my attention was distracted.

Rolle Dollar came in and laid a blacksnake whip on Sharniki's cigar counter, looked intently at Walter Ivy, then said, "I've not laid a whip on a man since I left Georgia." He spoke softly, slowly, drawling the words out, like they do all the time, and suddenly it was very quiet in the place.

A bit of cigar ash fell from Mike Sharniki's smoke and I swear I heard it hit the floor.

Walter Ivy laid his pool cue aside, but kept his hand on it. "You're not going to whip anybody, Rolle," he said.

—4

Rolle Dollar was a very tall man and extremely thin as though he were wasted by some undefinable disease. Yet he was a strong man; we all knew that, for he had bodily thrown rowdy cowboys out of his hardware store from time to time. I had never liked the man; his eyes were set close together and bracketed a long, bony nose and he always gave me the impression that his opinion was more valuable than anyone else's.

"There was no call to talk to Mrs. Dollar the way you did," Rolle said. "I won't have any man speaking lies to my wife. Sinful lies. I'll pray to God to wipe out this sin on your soul, Walter Ivy." He slid the whip off the cigar counter and spread ten foot of it out behind him.

There wasn't anyone there who didn't know what a blacksnake could do; an average man skilled in handling one was more than a match for a proficient gunman and could cut a man to the bone before he could unlimber his pistol.

Walter Ivy was unarmed and Rolle Dollar knew it, but as I said, it wouldn't have made any difference. Mike Sharniki put both hands on the counter and said, "Rolle, I wouldn't start nothin' was I you."

"I'm the hand of God," Dollar said. "No man need tell me what to do." He watched Walter Ivy with his narrow-eyed stare and Buford Brittles got up and slid back his chair. "Keep out of this, old man."

"Intend to," Brittles said and put both hands on the back of his vacated chair and stood that way. He was a grizzled bear of a man with massive shoulders and drooping waterfall mustaches and jaws that worked unceasingly on his chewing tobacco.

I thought it was a muscle twitch in Dollar's shoulder that tipped Buford Brittles off, or it could have been the instinct born of past bad trouble. Anyway he moved faster than I ever thought a man his age could move and he flung the chair, not at Dollar, but up and where the whip would catch into it, tangle around the rungs.

The chair, caught in the whip, crashed into Sharniki's showcase and brought it down in splinters, showering cigars and pipe tobacco and cut plug all over the floor. And before Rolle

43

Dollar could free his whip and set it again, Walter Ivy bounded for him.

He grabbed Dollar and flung him back against the wall where he hit a rack of pool cues. He lost his whip and bounced off the cues and he half fell in his attempt to get out of Ivy's way.

But there was no getting out of the way for Ivy snatched up the whip and raked it out behind him. With a bleat of fear, Rolle Dollar made for the front door and his feet just passed over the threshold when Ivy caught him around the ankles and sprawled him headlong across the boardwalk.

The noise was attracting a crowd and men boiled out of Mulligan's saloon, eager for anything to break the monotony of a dull, hot night. Rolle was on his hands and knees, trying to get up in a hurry but then Walter Ivy gave him the whip on the cracker-thin buttocks, renting Dollar's trousers and drawing blood.

His yell could be heard all over town and he went flat on the walk and Ivy hauled back and dusted the other buttock, again ripping the cloth and inflicting a deep wound.

Dollar, like most merciless men, was pleading for what he had always denied others.

Yet I felt sorry for him and said, "That's enough, Walter!"

"Just a couple more," he said coldly and made it good. Then he threw the whip into the street and said, "Go sew the sonofabitch up, and if you use anything but a dull needle we'll have words over it."

With that he turned and walked back into the pool hall as calmly as though he had just stepped out to take the night air.

He had, I'm sure, exhibited a side of his nature that none knew and few suspected. But it was something they all understood, a man sticking up for his rights and defending himself when he had to.

But there wasn't time for me to ponder the mores of Texas justice; there was a badly hurt man sprawled and crying on the boardwalk. I helped him to his feet, wishing that he had been injured some other place so he could have ridden the six blocks to his house.

Blood was running down the backs of his legs and soaking his shredded trousers and the sight of Rolle Dollar, buttocks exposed, excited sympathy in me and I looked around.

"Won't one of you loan me a vest? Anything to wrap around him."

One of the T-Cross cowboys laughed and said, "Goin' bare-assed won't hurt him none, 'cept his damned pride and he's got too much of that already."

They weren't going to help any; I could see that, so I went on down the street with Rolle Dollar, thankful that it was dark and that there were but a few people downtown. We had to go

45

past the hotel and the newspaper and the store was across the street and the ladies turned away as we passed and spared Dollar that.

When I got him to his house, his wife did just what you'd expect her to do; she gave one unholy cry and fainted. The commotion got Angeline out of bed and she came down as I was stretching Rolle face down on the horsehair sofa and opening my bag.

She saw his distress and rushed to him. "Papa!" Then he hit her. "Jezebel!" he shouted. "Harlot!"

It was a thing that could make a man's best intentions go out the window and out of mind; I had been uncorking the ether bottle and then I put the cork back in it, slipped it back into the bottle pocket of my bag and put eighteen sutures in his bottom, each one done right, and each one a separate agony. Then I dressed him and turned to his wife, who was stirring and trying to sit up; she certainly had missed the bad part. Getting Rolle up the stairs to his bed was no problem; he was angry enough to make it under his own steam and his wife went with him, heaping solicitude on him and Rolle kept shoving her away.

I made Angeline sit down and put a cold pack on her cheekbone; she'd have a nice bruise all right. Upstairs Rolle was ranting and quoting Scripture; it was a frightful din, and with the windows open the neighbors must have heard everything.

"Sometimes I'm so ashamed," Angeline said softly and made a study of her fingers laced together. "Why? That's what I keep asking myself. Why do people want others to live in fear of them?"

In one of those flashes of insight, I said, "I suppose it's because they are so afraid themselves that they can't trust others to be kind or thoughtful or fair." Then I told her what had happened; it was better that I tell her than to let her get it from gossip, and surely the whole town would be talking about it. Perhaps it was just the thing to take their minds off the drought and let tempers cool a bit.

"I'm ashamed of myself because this was all my fault," Angeline said. "But I—I didn't want to fight Lunsford Cardine. That's sinful isn't it? I mean, one thing leads to another, doesn't it? I suppose it'll get all over town, what I did."

"Now I don't think it'll come to that," I said, not too sure myself, but I was sure I should convince her if I could. "Lunsford is a gentleman, isn't he?"

I didn't get an answer and that left me with a little worry of my own; her mother came down the stairs, her eyes red from crying.

"Barbaric," she said, "that's what it is. Barbaric!"

"If you're talking about Mr. Dollar's conduct," I said, "I would have to agree. Good night, madam. I'll drop in day after tomorrow and check his

47

condition. He may run a slight fever, but I wouldn't concern myself about it. Also his appetite may subside, but I'd try to get some broth in him anyway." I gave her four pills; my oath overcoming my personal feelings. "These, taken as directed, will help ease his pain and allow him to sleep."

She took the pills, then said, "I'm going to have a warrant sworn out, mark my words!"

"That would be ill-advised," I said, smiled at Angeline, and walked out, trying to visualize what it would be like to have Rolle Dollar for a father-in-law.

And I just couldn't. Some things are too horrible to contemplate.

I was sleeping when the sheriff and his posse came back and woke me; it was a quarter to four in the morning and I fumbled for the lamp and then Walter Ivy came in, his eyes puffed with sleep. "I'd like to use your examining room, Ted." Without waiting for an answer he opened the door and went in and lit the lamps, then called to the sheriff, who was outside: "Bring her in here, Ben. Handle her gentle there. Right there on the table."

I stepped in and the men with the sheriff put the girl on the examination table. She was incredibly dirty, as though she had never known a bath. Her dress was torn and she was barefoot.

Ben Titus shooed his deputies outside and Walter Ivy looked at me. "Why don't you and Ben wait outside? Get the gist of this if you can, Ted."

I resented it a little, being pushed out of my own examining room, but I didn't want to make an untidy issue of it so I stepped outside with Sheriff Titus. He found the stub of a cigar in his pocket and lit it. Dust lay heavy in the creases of his clothing and he was unshaven and tired.

"Cut Comanche sign day before yesterday," he said softly, running the words together. "Followed 'em north but never caught up with 'em until dawn this mornin'. Found a camp somewhere west of Gonzales. We hit 'em hard and sudden. When the dust settled there was five dead and the girl."

"She's white," I said.

Ben Titus nodded. "Yep. White all right. Some buck took her in a raid, probably north of where we found 'em. From their looks I'd say they'd been travelin' some, and movin' fast. Figured that when we caught 'em camped in the open that way. Indians don't take chances unless they're about run out."

He turned to his deputies who stood idle nearby. "Why don't you go home now and get some sleep? And I don't think any of this is worth a lot of talk now, if you understand what I mean."

"Sure, Ben."

"We understand, Ben."

They walked off, leading their horses, dragging themselves because they were tired. Ben Titus puffed on his cigar and waited and then Walter Ivy stepped outside.

"Well, Doc?" Titus asked.

"She's resting under sedation," Ivy said. "Ted, do you have a cigar? Thank you." He cupped his hands around mine when I offered a match and his face was drawn and angry. "I think I can draw a few safe conclusions for you, sheriff. She's perhaps nineteen and she was taken just a few days ago. I deduce that from the condition of her feet; they're bruised and cut and not yet healed. It's my opinion that she's German, probably from the colony up around Fredericksburg."

Titus nodded. "I guess there ain't no sense in me askin'—Comanches only take a woman for one thing."

"Yes, but the less said about it the better," Walter Ivy said. "Do you think you can locate her family, Ben?"

"Don't seem like much sense to try, Walter. I used to deputy up in that part of the country and them Germans are strange ones. From her clothes I'd say she was a bound girl to begin with."

"Sheriff, that's ridiculous!" I put in. "We don't have bound girls in this day and age."

He smiled at my ignorance. "They're furriners, Doc. Got their own ways of doin' things. Yep,

50

she's bound. And now that she's been used they ain't likely to take her back, fearin' of course that she'll up and fetch a breed in time. Them furriners are funny."

"The possibility of pregnancy exists," Ivy said, "although I think it unlikely in this case. Well, Ben, we've got to do something with her."

"Figured you'd know what," Titus said. "Good night."

"Wait now," Ivy said, but Ben Titus was walking away with no intention of stopping or turning back.

Walter Ivy slapped the back of his neck and said, "Now isn't that a hell of a note?" He blew out a long breath and made a decision. "Go and wake Mrs. Hempstead and while you're at it, heat a couple of kettles of water. Mrs. Hempstead can help me bathe her and we'll get her into a spare bed." He looked at me and suddenly flung out his hands in a helpless gesture. "Well, what the hell do you expect me to do with her?"

Her name was Christina Heidler and I am to this day unsure just how she became my patient, but Walter Ivy, with his vast cleverness, managed to arrange it. She remained for a week in our small hospital while her feet healed and her spirit repaired the damage of the barbaric assault.

She spoke good English, although with some accent and she was a bright girl, rather pretty in a large-boned way, but not heavy fleshed as I thought most German girls were.

I felt it was Ivy's duty to give her a complete physical examination but he fended it off to me, saying that he had a call to make north on the Guadalupe and that was the last I saw of him for three days.

Christina Heidler had her mind pretty set on "that other doctor" and it looked for a time as though the examination would have to be postponed. She felt that I was too young to be a doctor and of course this annoyed me to no end, and aroused my determination to carry this thing through.

I could see that we weren't going to get along at all; she argued, balked, protested, and argued some more and I rapidly lost patience to the point where I told her that if she had hurt her hand she would expect the doctor to examine it, and since she had been injured—she grasped my point immediately.

People can be cooperative when they want to.

Still, with Walter gone and Christina quite able to leave, I was faced with a decision, one that Walter really should have made. But I was still smarting a little and decided to arbitrarily take this on myself and I offered her a job as nurse, two dollars a week and room and board. Certainly it seemed a logical solution for in the past we had had to tend our hospitalized patients ourselves, or foist it off on

Mrs. Hempstead, who was a little cross at times.

I felt that we needed a nurse and Christina was intelligent and strong and we could teach her and before long she would be quite capable of tending bed-ridden patients while we went our rounds.

It all sounded very brilliant and I was sure Walter Ivy would approve.

This decision was made on Friday, October 25, and it turned out to be one of the hottest days we had had, and one of the most tragic. I don't think anyone ever figured out why it happened, and only a few knew how, but it was Spindle's day in town and everything seemed normal, or as normal as could be expected with the tension between the brands.

Then Bob Scourby, who was the ramrod for T-Cross, got it into his noggin that he could ride into town any day he pleased and he got seven men who agreed with him. So, bolstered by a bottle of whiskey, Scourby took his men and this desire for independent expression and rode into Victoria, just looking for trouble.

They tied up at Mulligan's saloon, and since Spindle horses crowded the hitchrack, they solved this untidy parking problem by turning all the Spindle horses loose. Then they paraded inside, ordered in loud voices, and declared that any man who wasn't a hog with his water was welcome to drink.

Tennessee Frank, who ran Spindle, was a man

of proud and sensitive stock and immediately took umbrage at the remark and demanded to know what Scourby meant.

Mulligan swears Scourby reached for his starboard pistol first and Tennessee Frank, proving once and for all that his reputation was more than talk, promptly drew and shot Scourby dead, then seriously wounded a cowboy standing next to him.

At the precise time the first shots were fired, I was in Angeline Dollar's parlor, inquiring about the state of her health and thinking unprofessional things.

The walls of the house muffled the shooting somewhat, but I knew it was more than some wrangler letting off steam and I grabbed my bag and tore out of the house.

—5

The shooting continued as I ran for the main street; it sounded like a squad practicing at the rifle butts, and as I rounded the last corner, the swamper from Mulligan's was out in the street yelling for a doctor.

I'm not sure what I expected when I barged into the saloon, but certainly not what I found. Bob Scourby was dead and so were three of his men.

Another lay against the brass footrail, one hand draped inelegantly in the spittoon; he had a horrible wound in his neck. Two lay in the bloody sawdust and one blew pink froth past his lips when he breathed; a lung wound for sure.

Tennessee Frank was down with three bullets in him, but he was alive. A dead man was sprawled across his legs and Mulligan helped me get him off. Two Spindle men were beyond help and another sat against an upended table top, his empty pistol in his lap; both hands clutched a stomach wound.

"Go get some help," I said to Mulligan. "A dozen men! Tear down some doors to carry these men! Get a wagon!" I had perhaps a dozen other instructions but he dashed out and cut me off.

There were at least thirty Spindle riders standing in the saloon, staring dumbly at the sudden destruction; many of them had not fired a shot and later I decided that only a few—the dead and wounded—had been quick enough to get into the fight before it was all over.

But they were the men I needed and I shouted them into action; they tore off the tops of Mulligan's poker tables and we began to carry the wounded outside. Ben Titus was running down the street toward us; he took it all in at a glance and saved his questions for later.

"There's dead men inside," I said and Ben Titus nodded.

"That's my department," he said and I hurried on toward my office.

Christina Heidler was making up some beds in the hospital room when I rushed in. "There's been a shooting," I said, then further qualified that. "Get four beds ready. You'll have to help me the best you can. It's all we can do."

All we can do; I'll never forget that phrase.

There is no use in trying to describe what happened in its natural sequence, or to relate what the sheriff did, or others did, because they had their work and I had mine and I just had to stop and gather myself and fight down the instinct to do everything at once.

A doctor can't do that. He has to take things one at a time, make up his mind as to who needs help the worst and then do what he can.

That damned phrase again.

I had Tennessee Frank brought into the operating room. One bullet had broken his thigh six inches above the knee but I gave that only a passing attention. He was also wounded high in the chest, a serious enough thing, but not something likely to cost him his life.

Frank was unconscious and I incised his lower abdomen, knowing as I did so that his chances were slim; abdominal wounds of this nature carried high risks and while I had Christina spraying carbolic acid to kill bacteria, the terror of peritonitis lurked like a shadow behind us.

The bullet had perforated the lower intestine, and with artery forceps to control hemorrhaging, I sutured and hoped for a little luck. Tennessee Frank's other wounds were serious enough and I probed and found the bullet in his chest; it was a .36 caliber from a Navy cap-and-ball pistol and had not penetrated deeply enough to be fatal.

The bullet in his thigh was removed and once he was in traction, Christina and I wheeled him into the hospital room and transferred him to a bed.

By my watch an hour and fifty-one minutes had passed.

Buford Brittles was outside, and all of his men and at least twenty-five people from town. He looked immeasurably sad and said, "How's Tennessee, Doc?"

"He may make it, if he's lucky."

Someone had thoughtfully pulled a blanket over the other Spindle rider and Buford said, "He died not ten minutes after he was brought here. I guess you've done all you could for us."

His tone, hard, unrelenting, the tone of a man pushed to the limits of his control made me say, "Buford, I don't want any more patients, you understand?"

"A man's got to take things as they come," he said and turned away, pushing through the crowd and taking his riders with him.

I had the T-Cross man with the lung wound brought in, and when I was through and he was resting in bed under sedation, I tended to the last of the living participants in this madness.

Once cleaned, his neck wound was more ugly than serious and after cleaning it and staunching the bloodflow, I bandaged him with a compress and got him into bed with a pain killer.

He wanted whiskey but I held out for an injection.

Somehow I had lost track of the passage of time and then I noticed sunlight slanting through the west windows and realized that the day was about gone and there would be a long night ahead of me. The operating room was a mess and I went outside, got two pails of water and fixed a fire to heat them. Christina came from the adjoining room and eased the door closed. Her dress was bloody and so were her hands and perspiration soaked her shoulders and bosom.

"You don't rattle easily, do you?" I said.

"What is this, 'rattle'?"

"Faint. Get frightened."

She shook her head. "Nothing can frighten me." Then she sighed. "You rest. I'll clean."

"We'll both clean," I said and got the mop.

It was almost dark by the time we were through and each had bathed and changed clothes. When I stepped outside my room I noticed that a slight breeze had sprung up; it stirred the trees and the dead, sun-killed grass and swirled flavors of the earth into the air.

Ben Titus came down the street, his gait plodding. When he saw me sitting on the stoop, he stopped and said, "Three alive. Nine dead. God, that's a waste! Good men too. A couple had families."

"Tennessee is in bad shape," I said. "Whether he pulls through or not is up to God. I did all I could, but—" I shrugged. "The infection is what he'll have to fight off, and I can't help him."

"When's Doc Ivy coming back?"

"Tonight, maybe, if the stage gets in on time." Christina came out and nodded politely, then sat down beside me. She had changed to a clean cotton dress and her tawny hair, damp from her bath, was tied back with a ribbon.

"Feelin' all right there, girl?" Ben Titus asked. She looked up quickly, knowing what he meant, then Titus smiled. "One thing you got to understand about my deputies is that they're good for nothin' except possein' now and then and they get three dollars a day, which is about all the honest money they'll ever earn. Of a consequence they do what I say, and say what I tell 'em to say. Folks around here have come to understand that you came here hired by Doc Ivy and Doc Bodry here. We can let it go at that if it's all the same to you."

I was watching her face and her eyes and she gave no indication that she was going to cry. The tears just spilled over and ran down her cheeks and she nodded her head and kept nodding for a moment, then Ben Titus cleared his throat, turned, and walked back toward the center of town.

"Old Ben now, after spending half his life chasing rustlers and such, you wouldn't think—" I stopped talking because Christina grabbed my hand and pressed it against her cheek then kissed it and quickly got up and ran inside, leaving me wondering what it was all about.

Since Dorsey wasn't feeling well and Mrs. Hempstead was in one of her grumpy moods, I decided to go uptown and have supper in the hotel. But I first went to the back where Christina had her room and knocked lightly. I heard her speak and pushed the door open. She had been stretched out on the bed but she sat up quickly.

"I'm going uptown for perhaps an hour. Look in on the patients and if anyone stirs, come and get me right away. All right?" She nodded and I winked and closed the door.

When I reached the main street I found Buford Brittles and all the Spindle riders mounted and clogging the street. Ben Titus was there, and Aaron Stiles from the paper; they had been talking to Buford and stopped when they saw me come up.

The wind was picking up in strength and it seemed to sway him a little as he sat his horse. "Ted," he said, "I'll tell you what I've already told the others: I've had enough. Tonight I ride on T-Cross."

"Buford," Titus said, "there's no call to do that." He reached up as though to touch Brittles' horse, then let his hand drop. "There are dead men on both sides. It should end there."

"I've worked as hard as any man for what I've got," Brittles said. "Fought for it too. I won't be set upon by another brand, Ben. I won't be made to apologize because I had the foresight Scully Beachamp lacks."

"You can't ride a man down," I said. "Buford, I've known you to be a fair man. Rough, granted, but as fair as I've seen. If I could, I'd stop you."

"Man, I've toasted under this cursed sun as much as any man and I've stepped backward to keep T-Cross and Spindle apart. But tonight tears all, by God. I can no longer trust Beachamp because he can't control his men." He made a motion with his knees and his horse backed, then he turned and his men turned with him and rode slowly from town.

I took Ben Titus by the arm. "Aren't you going to stop him?"

"How?" Titus asked and went down the street to his office.

I would have gone back too, only I remembered what I had come to town for and decided there was no need starving. So I went to the hotel and ate pot roast, then had the cook box a supper, which I took back to Christina. She was sitting on the stoop when I came down the street; I could see around the corner of the building and there were lights on in the Ivy parlor and I could hear the soft strains of the pump organ.

"I know you didn't get any supper so I brought you this," I said, handing her the cardboard box. She broke the string and opened it and began to eat.

"The wind's coming up strong, isn't it?"

"It's certainly a break in the heat," I admitted. There didn't seem to be any point in my telling her that there would be more killing before morning; she'd had enough to put up with. "In my spare time I want to teach you what you must know to be a good nurse. And I have a number of books I want you to read." I let a little silence run on.

"Christina, are your parents both gone?"

"Yes. Nine years ago."

"Any brothers or sisters?"

"Many, but they have families of their own and were poor. I lived with a friend of my father's but he could no longer keep me. His children were growing and could do my work, so I was bound to a man named Stutzmann. The Comanches killed him and his wife."

"Do you want to go back to Fredericksburg? That's where you're from, isn't it?"

"I don't want to go anywhere," she said. "I'd

rather stay here. If it's all right. I don't think Mrs. Hempstead likes me. She is German and another woman around—well, she thinks I will take her place. That's not so."

"I'll reassure Mrs. Hempstead," I promised. "She's a nice woman and I know you'll get along once she understands that you're only helping in the hospital." I patted her hand. "You get some sleep. I'll stay up and wake you when I get tired."

"You should sleep," she said, but got up because obedience was a strong habit with her. I thought she was going inside, but she paused with the door open. "Will you promise me something?"

"If I can."

"If I have a child, promise you'll kill it."

It is hard to put into words how much this shocked me. "I can't do that, Christina. And you don't know you're—well, Dr. Ivy doesn't think so."

"How can I bear to wait until I know?" she asked, then went inside before I could attempt to answer.

Sitting alone there on the step, I realized how well she had hidden her inner anguish and her shame although no blame for it could be laid on her. She was a calm girl and her trouble ran deep, held back, hidden; it would have been better if she had broken down and wept and given vent to the emotion bottled up within her.

But I didn't think she would do that, and it was

too bad. It occurred to me then that if Ben Titus and the posse hadn't found her she would have killed herself at the first opportunity. Many white women taken by Indians did just that, and many a Texan, before being killed himself, put a bullet into his woman's head to keep her from being taken to the blanket by a Comanche or Kiowa buck.

I stayed up until a little after two, then went to Christina's room and gently shook her awake, then went outside to wait while she dressed. There was really not much for her to do; I had done most of it, and nursing is a messy business. The cowboy with the bullet wound in the neck was restless and I had to tie him in bed, then he had an involuntary urination and I had to untie him and change the bed clothes.

Tennessee Frank rested as well as could be expected and the T-Cross rider with the lung wound seemed to be holding his own. My instructions were simple, to keep them covered, for the night was turning off chilly, and to watch the lung wound and wipe away any blood that appeared on the nose and lips.

Hemorrhage there was my big worry for if he started to thrash about and bleed internally, he was a dead man and I couldn't help him. Opening the chest surgically almost always proved fatal; the shock of the operation could not be counteracted due to the length of the procedure.

It wasn't until I stretched out on my bed that I realized how exhausted I was and for a time it seemed that I just couldn't sleep. But I did, and slept soundly. So much so that when I woke, it was with a snap; I sat up in bed, certain that someone had called me. Then I heard it again, Christina's voice and I went out, not bothering to pull on a shirt.

As I went through the examining room I became conscious of another sound, like the beating of a thousand small bird wings, then I saw her standing outside by the open door and the rain was pouring down, sheets of it, hammering at the parched ground until it rained a mist.

She was soaked to the skin and holding up her arms to let it run down the length of them, then I stepped out and let it beat against my face.

There is something glorious in a rain after a long dry spell; it seems to soak into the skin and fill the body with strength and renewed hope. The sky was melting, draining torrents and then I put my arms around her and brought her inside and closed the door. She leaned her back against it and pulled her shoulders up until she had no neck and water dripped off the hem of her dress and she closed her eyes and smiled and it was the first time I had ever seen her do that.

The first time she had shown genuine happiness, and it was then that I stopped worrying about her.

At dawn the rain stopped and the sun came out, bright through the clouds, and water dripped from eaves and muddied the ground and the streets and no one minded at all.

I went uptown early to have my breakfast and to inquire at the hotel about the stage, which was a good fourteen hours overdue now. The agent had heard nothing, so I walked four blocks down to the telegraph office, thinking there might be a message. Ben Titus was there writing out a message; he handed it to the telegrapher.

"You get an answer to that, Curley, I'll be in my office or at home." He smiled and took my arm, saying, "Want a word with you, Doc."

"This came for you a half hour ago," Curley said, handing me a telegram.

Dr. T. Bodry
Victoria, Texas

Make apologies to Dorsey . . . affairs have taken me to Abilene . . . will return in week or ten days . . . know you can carry through. . . .

Walter

"Hope that ain't bad news," Ben Titus said.

"No, Walter's just chasing rabbits again."

He frowned. "What does that mean?"

"Never mind. What did you want to see me about, Ben?" We left the telegrapher's place and walked slowly along. The boardwalks were swollen and as we stepped along, moisture oozed up around the nails.

"I was goin' to come to your office," Titus said, "but I knew you had enough problems of your own. Buford Brittles rode into town not fifteen minutes ago. He was alone. Came to my office. Just walked in, said nothin', took his gun and laid it on my desk and told me he would never touch a firearm again."

"My God, he didn't go through with it?"

Titus shook his head. "Nope. He was in the yard and he'd called Scully Beachamp and his family out, announced his intentions and lit the torch." He looked sideways at me. "Then it started to rain. I guess it was the coincidence, the knowledge of what he was going to do, and the rain, but anyway Buford just up and figured that God had reached out and spared him. He's over at the church now, talkin' to the parson and Rolle Dollar." He shook his head again. "I looked in there on my way to the telegraph office. Buford is kneelin' and prayin'. He up and took religion real serious."

"I wouldn't dispute that the rain was Providential,

Ben. Too bad it couldn't have come a day earlier."

"How's Tennessee and the others comin', Doc?"

"A day or two will tell one way or another." We had come to my turn off; I stopped a moment and we talked about generalities, then I walked on back to my office.

I was disappointed that the stage hadn't arrived because I was expecting some medical journals and some books. Doctors ruin their eyes reading, then ruin their health staying out at odd hours in all kinds of weather putting into practice what they've read.

Being a doctor was, to many, some kind of a pinnacle reserved for a special kind of man, and I suspect they were right; it takes a special kind of man who can bear the eternal burden of helplessness, for with every cure a doctor could effect there were a dozen instances where he had to stand back and watch his patient die. My large interest was surgery, and the strides being made in that field; it seemed to me to offer the most hope for the suffering, and each day, each year, hitherto unbreachable barriers were scaled, and in my own brief career, I had seen new skills added. During my first year at medical school, tumors were nearly always terminal, but in five years antiseptics and sepsis had made possible prolonged operations; personally I had excised tumors of the neck, ovarian tumors, vesico-vaginal fistula, and amputation of the cervix uteri, and in all cases saved patients from a terminal condition.

None of these things were without risk to be sure, but with cocaine and digitalis and chloroform, and the success in most instances of blood transfusion—although some patients died unexplainably—it was possible for me to perform a tracheotomy, or gall bladder operation, or the removal of the spleen, and Ceasarean section did not automatically mean the death of the mother.

This was, in my own mind, the large difference in thinking between Walter Ivy and myself; he was a doctor who believed that surgery was the last resort and much of his reading concerned drugs and treatment medicinally. Walter had a great interest in bacteriology and it was his everlasting interest in microscopic examination of specimens that broadened my own powers of diagnosis and firmly wedded in my own mind the association of scalpel and microscope.

Walter Ivy's sudden decision to remain away caused all of us to make some adjustments. Dorsey's temper was strained considerably, due more I think to her condition and the fact that she was feeling poorly much of the time.

I was a bit put out myself because I had to take on the added load of Walter's patients, but then I had done this before and it merely meant a little less sleep for me. All this meant that I had to sit down and devise some kind of a schedule in order to get everything done.

My patients in the hospital were recovering nicely and within ten days they were sitting up and eating so heartily that I had to call on Buford Brittles and Scully Beachamp for some kind of financial assistance.

They were again the best of friends, both sorry for their hard words and they both understood the delicacy of my mission, which was in essence, presenting a bill before the patients were discharged from my care.

The upshot of it was that both Beachamp and Brittles settled with me in full and I walked rather light-headed to the bank with a little over three hundred dollars in cash in my pocket.

Lunsford Cardine was minding the window; I presented my bank book and the money, holding out twenty dollars to pay the grocery bill. He made his entries, handed the book to me and said, "I want a word with you, Bodry."

His tone was the same as always and I still didn't like it. "What about?" I knew that he was still seeing Angeline Dollar on the sly.

"It's come to my attention that you've been paying a good deal of attention to Miss Dollar."

"So?"

"So I don't like it," Lunsford said. "And I like it less since that frump came to live with you. The whole town's talking about it."

I could feel my temper deep in the bowels, building, rumbling, rising to escape and I placed both hands firmly on the counter. "Lunsford, let me tell you something educational: Do not ever repeat that, to me or anyone else. If you do I'll pound your stupid head off."

Then I picked up my bag and walked out; I was afraid to remain longer and as I walked toward the store to pay my bill, I wondered what made me so angry, the insult to Christina or the implication that I was hopelessly in love with Angeline Dollar. Although I had seen a good deal of her since her illness, I had to admit that there were facets of her personality that I disliked. She had a coyness that was irritating and she had the habit of always speaking depreciatingly about herself in the hope that I would leap to her defense.

That can get tiresome after a time.

And her mother was an abomination, conversationally anyway, and her father I would as soon not discuss; I simply disliked him as a man and abhorred him as a patient.

The rain came again, in the middle of the next week, a nice sprinkle that convinced everyone that the dry spell was really over. Grass was perking up and the creeks were partially full and the town settled down again and even the Indians stopped raiding, a blessing if there ever was one.

November came with colder mornings and I

71

kept busy with my patients and my reading and two hours each day I taught Christina Heidler the rudiments of nursing.

It is amazing what you can learn about a person without half trying. She had a good education, having completed the first eight grades of school and two of high school, an unusual thing for a girl in those days. Her ability to read German made some of my old textbooks quite useful to her, and with a mentality that was far above average, she soon became increasingly valuable to me, and patients whom I had never dared bring to my office and hospital were promptly popped into bed and cared for properly.

I got a letter from Walter; he raved about Abilene and during his stay he had been deluged with patients. He ended with a promise to return, but I knew Walter and didn't put too much stock in it.

Dorsey was pretty put out about it, and one evening when I came in from a call in the country, she came to my office before I could hang up my coat and wash my hands.

And she came right to the point. "I've written Walter all about the German girl."

"You mean, Christina?"

"You know exactly who I mean, Ted Bodry."

"Yes, I do," I said, sitting down. "What have you written Walter?"

"Don't pretend you don't know."

"I'm not pretending anything," I said, getting a little angry.

"I can't keep that girl here any longer," Dorsey said flatly. "I mean it, Ted. She has to go."

"Dorsey, you've never kept her at all. Her room and board is paid for out of my own pocket." I waved my hand to include the office and operating room and the three rooms behind, Christina's and mine, with the storeroom between. "I've always paid Walter rent on these rooms, Dorsey. None of it ever came out of his pocket. And Christina's no burden to Mrs. Hempstead; she cooks in her own room and washes her own clothes. As a matter of fact, Dorsey, I don't think Christina's ever once been inside your house. She wouldn't intrude on your privacy. And neither would I. So don't say that I have."

"Oh, you're so damned righteous!"

"Not intentionally. But I'm not guilty of anything either. Look, you're pretty upset with Walter gone so long and—"

"Don't patronize me!"

I drew in a deep breath and let it out slowly. "Just what is it you want me to do, Dorsey?"

"Get rid of that girl."

"I can't do that," I said. "She's a valuable pair of hands to me. Since she's been here I've been able to extend my practice, as well as take care of Walter's practice. And I've also performed three operations." I shook my head. "She's becoming too valuable to lose, Dorsey." I was tired of discussing it, justifying what needed no justification in my mind; I got up and went to the door and opened it. "I don't think there's anything more to be said, Dorsey. If you want, take it up with Walter. He can decide."

Her manner changed—perhaps she saw that I was adamant. "Oh, I hate him!" she said and began to cry, and I understood what her trouble was. So I made her sit down and gave her a shot of medical brandy and fifteen minutes later her attitude had brightened and she went back to the house and I walked downtown to the telegraph office. I wrote out what I wanted to say and handed it to the telegrapher, who read it, then looked at me sharply.

"You sure you want to say that, Doc?"

"Exactly that. How much?"

He read it, counting the words: Get . . . the . . . hell . . . home . . . where . . . you . . . belong . . . and . . . stop . . . acting . . . like . . . a . . . damned . . . underwear . . . salesman. . . . "Fifteen words, Doc; that'll be two-eighty."

I paid him and walked out while the telegrapher was clearing the line. Walter would be furious when he got that, perhaps furious enough to get on the next stage for Victoria! He wasn't fooling me any; a new town beckoned to him and he looked at the grass and was deciding whether or not it was really greener and unless I was mistaken, he had already wired friends in the east and offered to sell his Victoria practice.

He'd done it before and what a man will do once, he'll do again.

Tennessee Frank came in to see me the next day; his wounds were healing splendidly and I took the cast off his leg. We talked about the shooting and he acted as though he could hardly remember the sharper details of it and I suppose it was really that way, a bit of a blur in his mind, just a few shocking seconds of complete violence.

The two T-Cross riders were completely recovered and working again and I considered them completely discharged.

The next day, when the stage arrived, I went to pick up my mail and another package of journals. Walter and I were both fairly prolific correspondents, especially with other doctors, and Walter was always working on some paper to be submitted to the medical journals. I never bothered with it myself, but I had a friend practicing in Cincinnati who had been operating for tubal pregnancy and I was very interested in his technique and successes.

Of all the burdens of woman, tubal pregnancy stands in my mind as the most terrible. It sometimes happens that the embryo develops in the tube leading to the uterus and as it grows it ruptures the wall of this tube. Serious hemorrhage follows and the doctor is forced to watch the life ebb as a torrent of blood pours into the abdominal cavity and could not until now lift a hand to help her.

This misplaced pregnancy is uniformly fatal and even while I was in medical school, learned doctors discussed opening the abdomen and correcting the situation surgically, but no one was bold enough to risk the hazards. But it was inevitable that someone would; my friend from Cincinnati, who had been kind enough to diagram his technique and report his results to me.

Walter returned that night, riding all the way from San Antonio on a livery stable horse and I suppose it did his old cavalry soldier soul good to do so. He had the good sense to spend a couple of hours with his wife before coming to my office; it was after ten o'clock but I was there reading, waiting for him, certain that he would show up.

He came in, tanned and robust and he flopped in a chair and looked at me for a moment. "You know, I should be sore at you, Ted. What would people think if they read that wire?" Then he waved his hand and laughed and lit a cigar. "I was ready to come home anyway. That's a lively place, Abilene. People have money and they need a doctor. The nearest is the contract surgeon at Fort Phantom Hill."

"Decided to move?"

He looked at me a moment. "Would you mind, Ted?"

"Why should I mind?"

He seemed very surprised. "Why, because you'd be going with me. Wouldn't you?"

"I don't think so, Walter. I have a good practice here and I like it here."

"You'd like it there," he said quickly. "Come on now, think it over. I can get three thousand in cash for your practice."

"You've had offers?"

"Well, it doesn't hurt to try."

"What does Dorsey say?"

He laughed. "Dorsey goes where I go. One place is the same as another to her."

"She ought to get out more, make friends," I said. "Walter, I think it would be a mistake to move. We're established. It would only mean doing a lot of work all over again, like building a hospital. Besides, I've been meaning to ask you, if I can ever get you to light long enough, about buying some new equipment."

He laughed and waved his hand. "Ted, let's face it, you're a gadget man. I'm from the old school that believes what a doctor can't carry in his bag isn't worth having." He got up and stretched. "In the morning suppose we get together for an hour and you can bring me up to date on the general state of health. Want to talk to you about that German girl too." He winked and went out and it was a few minutes before I could get back to concentrating on my books.

77

——7

In the days that followed I kept waiting for Walter Ivy to say something about "that German girl" but he never did and I concluded that he had talked to Dorsey and she had told him of my firm stand on the matter.

Walter knew when to let well enough alone.

He resumed his rounds as though he had never been away at all and I slacked off a bit, catching up on some of my rest.

Or trying to.

Mrs. Dollar sent a boy with a note and asked me to call and I went to her house in the early afternoon. She was in the parlor; it was her throne room and of course we had tea and small cakes, which made me immediately suspicious because it just wasn't her nature to be generous.

"I would like you to recommend a good doctor," she said.

You learn not to get offended; I said, "Walter J. Ivy."

"Mr. Dollar would never permit him in the house; it would be useless to ask. I was referring to a doctor in some other town."

"Well, there's Dr. Radcliff in Goliad. And Dr. Baker and Dr. Kyle in San Antone. Are you ill,

Mrs. Dollar?" I waited a decent interval for her to answer, and when she didn't, I said, "Really, whatever you tell a doctor is in strictest confidence, and you must eventually confide in someone."

"The matter is much too delicate," she said flatly.

It was the kind of a thing that made a doctor sigh, this damned female modesty; it had fettered the progress of obstetrics for four hundred years.

"Madam, forgive my bluntness, but does this matter concern a pregnancy?" I watched her face, her expression, her eyes, and they told more than I had guessed. "Madam, does this concern Angeline?"

I had not suspected that she was so near the breaking point, but suddenly she fell to weeping and I could not stop her. So I went outside and saw some boys playing across the street and one came over at my whistle. I pressed a nickel in his hand and told him to run uptown and fetch Rolle Dollar, then went back into the house. Mrs. Dollar was sobbing and pressing a handkerchief to her mouth and I sat down and let her weep; she was a woman who felt sorry for herself most of the time and this likely did her a lot of good.

Rolle Dollar didn't waste any time getting home; he rushed into the house and sat down beside his wife and put his arms around her. He dried her tears and patted her shoulder and then he looked at me as though I were to blame for it all.

"God frowns on this shameful house," he said. "She is in the hands of the Devil."

I didn't want to get involved in that, so I steered another course. "Mr. Dollar, trouble always *seems* worse than it is. Since neither of you have taken me into your confidence, I would like to excuse myself from the matter. I've already recommended to Mrs. Dollar several fine doctors, and I take it from her inquiry that you plan to take Angeline to another town."

"My mortification and shame is too—"

"Damn *your* feelings," I snapped. "Man, your concern should be for the girl!" I forced myself to be calm, clinical. "She should be examined and placed under a doctor's care. The moral issues do not enter into the picture at all. The circumstances that produced this state may be regrettable, and entirely repugnant to you, but nevertheless she should have competent medical help. Now, do you wish me to withdraw from the case?"

"It'll be the talk of the town," Rolle Dollar said.

"Not from me," I assured him.

He was a man completely at a loss as to which way to turn. "Dr. Bodry, what do you advise? I don't know. On my soul, I just don't. For ten days now I've been in a daze, half out of my mind. I've always led a pure, Christian life, and now this—" He seemed too overcome to continue.

"I think, since you've asked, that we ought to face the facts. And fact one is that Angeline is pregnant. Fact two is that barring a miscarriage or complications, she will bear a child. It isn't something you can hide, Mr. Dollar. If you feel the shame is too great, then sell out and move to another town and tell everyone that her husband died. But at best that's risky. Texas is big, and yet it's small and soon the truth will come out. Someone will see you, or her; it's a thing that can't be hidden." I paused to let this sink in. "Point three is that you're going to have to have a doctor. Either myself or Dr. Ivy or some other physician. Your personal feelings don't matter, Mr. Dollar, and I sincerely suggest you consult Walter Ivy as soon as possible so that he can examine her."

"I've had words with the man," Dollar said, "and when I've had words with a man, I want no more to do with—"

"Mr. Dollar, you're not asking for treatment. It's Angeline we should be concerned with. Besides, neither Dr. Ivy nor myself have any choice, for by our sworn oath we can not refuse to treat anyone, any more than a priest can deny a man the right to confession." I picked up my hat and bag. "I would like for you to give what I've said serious thought. Please let me know."

Rolle Dollar nodded. "I talked to Butram Cardine and there'll be a wedding this Sunday. He's given me his word."

Since it's never a good policy to offer personal advice, I let myself out and went back to my office. By the time I reached the head of the block I knew something was wrong because four horses were tied up in front and there was a spring wagon there too, the bed full of straw, which meant that someone had been hauled in it.

I ran the rest of the way and met one of the Hulse boys; their father had a place about four miles out. He grabbed me and nearly towed me through my office and into the operating room. Guy Hulse, the youngest, lay like a dead man on the operating table and Christina was putting cold packs on his abdomen, which was badly lacerated and swollen. Old Peter Hulse and his other three boys crowded around and got in her way and I rudely pushed them aside.

"Pete, you stay. The rest of you wait outside. Git!" Then I looked at the old man and turned to examine the boy. He was young, eighteen or so, a big, healthy boy with a wrestler's shoulders. "What happened to him?"

"Horse fell and rolled on him," the old man said. "Is he gonna die, Doc?" He shifted his feet, making scraping sounds on the floor. "What makes him swell up like that? Is he busted up inside?"

There was no doubt in my mind that young Hulse was hemorrhaging badly internally, and I strongly suspected that he had a ruptured spleen.

I turned and immediately began to scrub up, giving rapid orders to Christina to prepare Guy Hulse for an immediate operation. His complexion was bad and I knew that I'd have to give him a transfusion.

"Pete, get out now, but send in your oldest boy. Alfy? Isn't that his name?"

"You going to cut my boy?"

"I'm going to try like hell to save his life, and I need Alfy. Now move. Every second counts."

Pete went out and Alfy came in; Christine had already brought a table close by and parallel to the operating table. "Lay down on that and strip to the waist, Alfy."

"Not in front of no woman I ain't," he said.

So I hit him in the mouth and it stung him and he blinked his eyes at me and did as he was told. Christina made ready to give the transfusion and I got the antiseptic sprayer hooked up and filled with diluted carbolic acid and began operating it with the foot pump. It was an untidy procedure, but it saved lives and that was all I cared about.

Alfy's eyes grew round when I found the vein in his arm and inserted the needle, but he didn't wince, and I adjusted the mixture of sodium phosphate which acted as an anticoagulant.

Christina acted as my anaesthesiologist, although the term was unknown in those days, and I made my first incision. She counted the patient's pulse and reported it to me in a calm, steady voice and

I gave my complete attention to my work. I could have used another nurse or a doctor to hand me instruments, but there was no one and I hated the seconds I wasted looking up at the tray beside me.

Alfy, whose blood ran from his arm into his brother's veins, started to say something, but Christina said, "Don't interrupt the doctor, Alfy."

Then she went on counting Guy Hulse's pulse and at the same time watching the chloroform breather very carefully, while I tied off the ruptures with forceps until I could tie off all the vessels. Working fast but carefully, I was ready to close in twenty minutes and I ordered the transfusion stopped.

Walter Ivy came in and I looked up. "Don't come in here without a scrub up," I said.

"Oh, for Christ's sake," he said and started to step.

"Damn it, Walter, I mean it!"

He looked at me steadily, then shrugged and walked out, closing the door. I discontinued anaesthetic and Christina helped me bandage the patient and we transferred him to a homemade gurney and moved him into the hospital room and into a bed.

I heard a thump in the other room and went back. Alfy was sitting on the floor, both arms outspread to brace himself. "I fell," he said.

"Let me get you some brandy," I said and

stepped out into my office. The Hulse family was there, with Walter Ivy. "He's no longer bleeding and his pulse is good. With luck now he'll be on his feet in two weeks."

The old man looked at the bottle in my hand. "If'n you're gonna get drunk, Doc, we'll go along with you."

"It's for Alfy," I said and went back in.

I just let him swig and he took three good swallows and it rooted color into his cheeks. He reluctantly handed the bottle to me. "That's good stuff, Doc."

"Why don't you take a couple of more swigs and get your strength back?"

"You sure know what you're doin'," he said and tipped the bottle again. I went into the hospital and Christina was making Guy Hulse comfortable, tucking the sheets in on each side so he wouldn't roll out.

"He'll be good and sick when he comes out of the chloroform."

She smiled. "I'll stay with him."

"Good," I said and went back to my office. The Hulses were outside with Walter Ivy; they were talking softly and quit when I stepped out. Alfy was tucking in his shirt tail and looking very bright eyed.

Old Pete Hulse shifted his feet and said, "He was bad hurt, huh, Doc?"

"Another hour and you'd have buried him," I

told him frankly. "The spleen was ruptured and filling the abdominal cavity with blood."

Old Pete nodded as though he really understood, and perhaps he did understand. "Alfy says you went and took his blood and run it into Guy's arm. Can you do that, Doc?"

"Yes, it's been done," I said. "Guy had lost too much blood by the time he got here and he wouldn't have survived an operation."

"How much of my blood did you take, Doc?" Alfy asked.

I shook my head. "I have no way of telling, Alfy. That's something we just haven't worked out yet."

The old man nodded; his son was alive and he was satisfied. "Doc, I only got eighty dollars in the bank, but I could give you fifty prime steers if that'd—"

"My fee is ten dollars, Pete. Pay me when you take Guy home."

He nodded once, and then turned to his wagon. His boys mounted up and turned out and I watched them go, feeling that this was one damned good day after all.

Walter Ivy stood there and when I started to go back into my office he said, "You got kind of short there, didn't you, Ted?" He followed me inside and perched on the edge of my desk. "I don't think I had that coming."

"Yes, I know that, Walter, and I apologize. It was

just that I'm on needles and pins when it comes to surgical sepsis. Perhaps even a little afraid. After all, the abdominal cavity was beyond the reach of surgery for so long that I still can't believe I'm being careful enough. The introduction of bacteria—" I waved my hand, terminating the explanation.

"I would have never given him a transfusion," Walter said. "Too many risks. Too many unknowns, Ted. There have been deaths."

"Yes, and they'll find out why. But he was going to die if I didn't get blood into him. I just couldn't stand by and watch that."

He sighed. "What are his chances?"

"Good, I believe. As good as Mrs. Miller after I removed her spleen." I couldn't hold back a smug smile. "And the last time I rode past her place I saw her hoeing weeds in the garden." The whiskey bottle was sitting on my desk, down considerable since Alfy had helped himself; I got two glasses and poured. "Walter, I'll tell you what I want to do. I'd like for us to get out of this building and put up another, a regular hospital."

"That would be a pretty big investment," he said, pursing his lips. "Now a lying-in hospital I can see. There's an advantage to that, Ted. Isolation for contagious diseases and care of the bed-ridden; there's a good revenue from that, Ted."

I looked at him. "And a small surgical room?"

"Well, yes. I don't think we should go overboard on surgery, Ted."

"Doctor," I said, "I would like to point out a thing or two. When a man has the bellyache or the croup he goes to his family doctor, but when he develops a cancer of the bowel, he goes to see a surgeon or an undertaker."

"Your point escapes me, Ted."

"The point is, they come to see the surgeon, traveling for miles, a hundred miles perhaps, if they know he can help them and has the facilities." I raised my hands and spread them out as though I were framing words chiseled in marble.

"Can't you see it? The WALTER J. IVY MERCY HOSPITAL?"

That got him off his butt and off my desk and he walked about, trailing cigar smoke, his eyelids pulled close together, his eyebrows shot up there in the vicinity of his hair. "I suppose you've looked into the cost of the building and equipment?"

"Yes, Walter, I have. A two storey building of brick would cost eight thousand dollars. Equipment, another ten. Expenses for operation for the first year, six more. That's twenty-four thousand dollars. I have a little over four saved. The rest would have to be borrowed, providing you matched me dollar for dollar."

He stopped pacing and looked at me. "Where would you put it?"

"On that three acre plot on the west edge of town, near the river."

"Who owns it?"

"Butram Cardine."

Walter Ivy smiled. "You've really put some thought into this, haven't you, Ted?"

"Would you like to see my sketches?" I got them out of a bottom drawer and he studied them at length, rocking back and forth on his heels.

"I like it," he said. "Ted, I really like it."

"As well as Abilene?"

He looked at me. "Where the hell's Abilene?" Then he laughed heartily.

—8

On Sunday, Lunsford Cardine, being a stinker with enough money to travel, left Angeline Dollar at the church, sobbing into her mother's bosom, and Rolle Dollar stalked the streets with a repeating rifle, looking for Cardine.

Fortunately, Ben Titus and three other men disarmed him and bore him, struggling and calling for vengeance, to his home.

And then I was summoned.

Titus felt that Dollar was making a big fuss over nothing; after all, Angeline wasn't the first woman jilted at the church, but then Titus didn't know the truth of the matter and no one was going to tell him either. I gave Rolle a sedative to quiet him and when he was resting, I went back to my office, in a way glad that he hadn't found Lunsford Cardine; Dollar would have killed him for certain and then Angeline would have been in a fine pickle.

On Monday I got on the stage for Austin. Since Walter wanted to get started on the hospital right away, I had to see an architect and have building plans made. Had we been building a hotel I wouldn't have bothered, but a hospital was different.

I remained in Austin for ten days and it was a relief; I hadn't realized how much I needed some time to myself and a little relaxation. Austin was quite a city and I went to the band concerts and the theatre and the music hall, figuring that it does a man good to watch pretty girls kick up their legs.

As it was good to get away, I found it equally good to get back and as the stage approached Victoria I wished the driver would let out the horses a little instead of poking along.

Ben Titus met me when I got off the coach; we drew aside to let other passengers and baggage unload. "Got a line on young Cardine," Ben said. "He's in El Paso. I ain't told Dollar yet."

"I wouldn't," I told him.

"Kind of thought I ought to keep it to myself," he said.

"Thanks anyway, Ben." My bags were on the porch and I got them and walked the few blocks over to my office and room in back. I changed to a clean suit, washed, and went into my office to look through my mail.

Christina Heidler heard me and opened the door of the operating room; her smile was a bright, spontaneous thing, and I said, "How is my patient?"

"Walking about. Not much, but a little." She held the door open for me and I stepped into the operating room and passed through to the ward. Guy Hulse had been moved to a corner bed and a screen set up, the reason being that there were two women patients. Mrs. Clayborn had slipped on a frosty porch and hurt her back and Walter Ivy had her in traction, which made her feel so much better. And Mrs. Huddleston had a badly fractured arm; a chunk of wood had flipped up while she had been chopping.

They were Walter's patients and I was cheerful and friendly but kept my nose out of their business. Guy Hulse was the picture of health regained; he sat up in bed, propped by pillows and he grinned when Christina and I stepped behind the screen.

"Pa says you whittled on me proper, Doc."

"Well, we did carve you a little. Sewed a little

too." I felt his pulse, strong and steady. "Been having visitors?"

"Sure 'nuff," Guy said. "But I can't fight with Alfy no more, Doc. With his blood running in me, it'd be like hittin' myself. And we used to have some real set-tos."

"Let me look at your scar." I examined him carefully; the healing was pink and firm, then I dropped the tail of his nightshirt. "Guy, I'm going to send you home tomorrow. But you stay off horses and no heavy work until I tell you. Don't carry wood or water. Understand?"

"Whatever you say, Doc."

"That's what I say." I motioned for Christina to follow me and we went back to my office. "Close the door." I waved her into a chair. "I've been thinking a lot about you, Christina. You're not pregnant, you know."

She looked steadily at me. "Yes, I know."

"You're young and pretty and healthy and some day a man is going to come along and you'll fall in love and get married. But until then you have a life of your own to lead. I want you to stay with Dr. Ivy and myself."

"Isn't it more you than Dr. Ivy that wants me to stay?"

"It may be now, but that can change. It will change, if it hasn't already. You've been taking care of his patients, you know. He can't sidestep that even if he wanted to." Then I told her of our plans to build a hospital, providing we could get the land and the financial backing. "Christina, I've grown fond of you, and I'm afraid in many ways, dependent on you. I want you to stay."

"Then I'll stay," she said.

I frowned and got up and walked around the small office. "Christina, I know you'll stay, but I keep getting the feeling that somehow I'm making you stay. That isn't what I want."

"I suppose that's true, but I'm the one at fault, not you." She waited until I looked at her. "Lying doesn't come easy to me, and pretending is something I never had time for, and I don't want to embarrass you, but I've done something I haven't a right to do. I've fallen in love with you."

I opened my mouth to tell her that she didn't know what she was saying, that she was mistaking gratitude for love; in short, all the stupid, vapid things men say when they are caught completely by surprise.

But I didn't say anything because she shook her head, asking me to be silent. "Please sit down," she said, and clasped her hands tightly together. "I'm sorry I said that. I thought it would be easier, but now I can see that it isn't. You'll remember that I said it and—" She acted close to tears. "Please, I would like to go away after all."

"Where would you go?"

She shook her head again, then said, "I don't know. Anywhere. It would be better, I know that."

I put my head in my hands for a moment, trying to organize my thoughts. "This is a devil of a mess—you know that? If I said anything at all you'd construe it as pity. If I told you that I was fond of you and needed you here, you'd think I was saying it to spare your feelings." I paused to light a cigar. "Damn it, Christina, give a man time to sort out his feelings, will you? Now that it's come down to it, I wonder why I was so set on your staying. Because I wanted a nurse or—"

"What else could it be?" she said quickly.

I studied her carefully. "Christina, don't be a *dummkopf*! Your experience may have stained you in the eyes of fools like Rolle Dollar, but not a man like me. Do you think for one second that I—" There was no sense getting into that. "You are going to stay. Clear?"

A lifetime of obeying commands was strong in her; she nodded her head. "Whatever you say." Then she turned and left my office and closed the door and I decided that I had accomplished absolutely nothing, and perhaps fogged up my own emotions good and proper. Now I wasn't sure how I felt and this made me unsure of myself, a status I didn't enjoy.

Butram Cardine fit my mental image of a banker, a rather smallish man who always wore conservative suits and sat behind his large walnut desk in a squeaky swivel chair.

All along I had thought that Walter would handle the negotiations, but he was called into the country and I went to the bank in his place. Cardine sat in his chair, tipping it back, squeaking it continually while I displayed the building plans and quoted figures. I noticed that when he had something to say he always stopped squeaking the chair, and he had a lot to say.

Nothing really suited him. The building was too large. There was too much equipment. He wanted to cut this and that and finally he had it pared down to practically nothing and he enjoyed every minute of it.

It was one of those times when you want very badly to tell a man where to put his money, but you dare not because you need him and he knows it and enjoys playing his games. The fact that both Walter and I were prepared to sink our total savings meant nothing to Cardine, and the meeting terminated dismally, with nothing at all being solved, or even close to being settled.

When I told Walter he was very disturbed about it and I got the impression that he felt I had lost my temper and botched it, although he didn't come right out and say so. A good thing too for I'd had just about enough for one day.

The only benefits derived from the meeting was that word soon got around town that we were planning a hospital; many spoke to me about it but I could promise them nothing.

It was all very discouraging.

At least until Thursday afternoon. I'd been out to the Stover place; the boy had fallen from a pear tree and hurt himself, but it turned out to be little more than severe bruises and when I tied up my rig in front of my office I noticed that Scully Beachamp's matched bays and buggy was soaking up the shade next to Buford Brittles' rig.

They were waiting in my office, smoking, talking softly, the best of friends now; they got up when I came in and we shook hands. I said, "Now neither of you looks a bit sick."

"Best of health," Beachamp said. "We heard talk about the hospital you and Doc Ivy want to build."

"That's about all it is, talk."

Buford Brittles said, "Heard you had plans drawn and everything. Wondered if we could take a look."

"I'd be happy to," I said and cleared the desk so I could spread the plans. I showed them the front and side elevation, then the first floor plan. "This is the entrance hall and Dr. Ivy's office and examining rooms are to the right. Mine are right across the hallway. On each side is a storeroom for drugs and dressings and general supplies. Directly in back is the emergency room, with surgery and recovery room right across the hall."

Brittles pointed. "Is that an elevator?"

"Yes, we'll need that for transporting bed-ridden patients to the second floor wards."

"That's going to be quite a place," Brittles said. "Take quite a few people to run it, won't it?"

I nodded. "In time, when it is operating to capacity, about sixty people."

Scully Beachamp whistled softly. "How much money do you need, Doc?"

"I—twenty thousand dollars," I said.

Brittles looked at Beachamp. "Halves?"

"Kind of figured that way." He offered his hand. "You want to go to the bank with us now?"

For a moment I was so stunned I couldn't speak. Then I said, "I think we need an attorney. Suppose I wire Austin?"

"All right," Brittles said, "but we shook on it. Let us know when he gets here." He put on his hat, ready to leave now. I got up and went out with them and watched them drive away. They were heading toward town when Walter Ivy came down another street in his buggy. When he pulled in and tied up, he said, "What did those two old war horses want?"

"They just loaned us twenty thousand dollars."

I enjoyed it, watching his eyebrows shoot upward, watching him swallow twice before speaking. "You're not joking?"

"About that much money?" I shook my head. "I'm going to wire a lawyer and have him draw up the papers. With luck, we should start building within a month."

"Still got your heart set on that piece of property west of town?"

I nodded. "There isn't a better spot around here, Walter."

"And Cardine owns it."

"Well, we'll just have to buy it from him."

"At his price?" Walter shook his head. "I think Mr. Cardine ought to donate that as a measure of his civic pride."

"Hell, he'll never do that!"

"Let me work on it," Walter said and walked around the house.

I didn't think any more about it until lodge meeting three nights later and then I noticed that Butram Cardine was getting the cold shoulder from Rolle Dollar and Mike Sharniki and a few of the other businessmen in town, but it wasn't until later that I found out just what was happening.

Walter had called at the bank and Cardine had quoted a firm asking price, which was plenty steep in any man's language, and Walter had told him he'd think it over.

Only Walter started talking it over with everyone in town and in a way that only Walter can talk. I could just hear him and see him by closing my eyes. He'd stand there with that bland, I'm-a-big-friendly-dog expression in his voice, saying, "Yes, sir, I wanted to put up the hospital on that land. Dr. Bodry picked it and you know how I feel about that young man. Salt of the earth. Give him my arm up to here. Bodry's done a lot for people around here and you'd think a man like Cardine would appreciate it, but does he? Just wants to make a dollar. Doesn't care how people have to suffer. It isn't *his* misery. It makes a man think about the money he keeps in that bank. For two cents I'd draw it out and do my business in Goliad."

Around town he'd go, making his rounds with cronies and friends and anyone who'd stop and listen, talking it up, never really saying anything bad but pretty much painting Cardine as a skinflint who'd take pennies from his mother's purse.

So Butram started getting the cold treatment at lodge and it kept up this way for nearly a week and I wondered when it would break. Cardine was a civic-minded man, with a finger in every-thing and I knew that he had the best interests of the community at heart. And because he was sincere, all this bothered him a lot and it was only a question of time before he broke down and sent a boy with a note, asking either or both of us to drop into the bank at our convenience.

We did, but I could see that the matter had already gone too far. I wasn't against paying a reasonable price for the land, but Walter Ivy had used his influence to the extent that Butram

Cardine had to give it to us outright or be forever remembered as a money-grabber by the townspeople.

Walter Ivy thought this was a grand gesture and promised Cardine that he'd put a bronze plaque in the cornerstone to remember this generosity; it was the wrong thing to say and Cardine was furious when we left the office and his anger was at me as much as at Walter and I couldn't blame the man for that because we'd been tarred by the same brush.

I spoke to Walter about it when we got into his buggy. "Damn it, you didn't have to push his nose in it that way. Why make an enemy of the man?"

"Hell, he was never a friend."

"A neutral is sometimes as valuable as a friend."

"My boy, listen to old Walter for a minute. The day will come when Butram Cardine will thank me for wresting from him this generous contribution." He patted me on the knee and clucked to the team and from his expression I could tell that he was certain everything was all right.

But I still wondered.

9

On Wednesday, November 26th, I got a wire from Dr. Calendar in Cincinnati, inviting me to spend ten days with him in a new surgical clinic he and a partner had established. I should have turned it down, with the foundation work beginning on the new hospital and patients to see, but I didn't hesitate at all; I wired back that I was taking the first available transportation to Austin and the railroad, and bought two round trip tickets to the hotel.

Walter Ivy was having his midday lunch with his wife and I walked around to the front entrance, knocked, and Mrs. Hempstead let me in. As I went toward the kitchen I realized that I hadn't been inside Walter's house for a long time.

He smiled and offered a chair when I came in. Dorsey was quite round now and her complexion was good although her disturbed body chemistry had given her a few pimples.

"I'm sorry to disturb you, Walter, but I want to go east for a few weeks." I explained the offer from Dr. Calendar. "It's something I can't afford to pass up, Walter, and you can handle my practice while I'm gone." I didn't remind him that I had handled his patients more than once.

"Well, I certainly don't begrudge you the opportunity," he said thoughtfully, "but with building going on and many details to look after, this could have come at a better time."

"Yes, I know. However I've made arrangements to go. I'm taking Christina Heidler with me."

Dorsey, who hadn't been paying too much attention, looked up quickly. "Really, Ted, together all that distance?" She looked at Walter, as though she expected him to say something. "You know how people talk."

"Yes, and isn't it a shame? However, I believe she can get some valuable training by observation," I said. "People are just going to have to go ahead and talk."

"Oh, they will," Walter said. He sighed and pushed back his empty plate. "Calendar, Calendar—oh, yes, he's that bright young man who's specializing in abdominal work. Risky business. He'll kill more than a few before he's through. Frankly, I'd rather they passed on in their own bed than on my operating table." He shook his head. "God, the war was bad enough. Died like flies the minute the stomach wall was punctured. Terrible risk, going in there. Broken bones are one thing, but I think a man's future lies in internal medicine. Correct the symptom before it develops, not surgery afterward." He sighed as though he argued a hopeless cause.

There was no sense of my staying; I got up and

replaced my chair. "This afternoon, Walter, if you could drop around to my office, I want to discuss several cases with you. I have Bert Caslin on digitalis; his heart's very bad. And there's Mrs. Ryker over at the junction; she's terminal cancer I'm afraid and it's merely a matter of sedating her to make her as comfortable as possible."

"I have some time around three," Walter said, so I smiled at Dorsey and left the house, feeling that I was certainly putting Walter to a lot of trouble. When I got around to my side of the house I saw Rolle Dollar walking back and forth, hands in his pockets, head down as though he wanted to observe each step he took.

He looked up when I drew near, then took my arm before I could step inside. "Doc, can you come to my house? Angeline's pretty sick."

"Of course. I'll get my bag."

He waited and we walked together and he hurried; it was really the first time I had ever seen him do that. Mrs. Dollar was in her usual state, wringing her hands and puckering her lips.

I went upstairs, alone; I insisted upon that. Angeline was in bed, and her complexion was bad although her pulse was strong. I questioned her briefly; she complained of severe pain in the abdomen and my first thought was the appendix, a trouble area we couldn't do much about.

But I went on with my examination and when I detected vaginal bleeding I knew what was wrong and went downstairs. I washed in the kitchen then went to the parlor where Rolle Dollar and his wife waited.

I suppose my expression gave away the seriousness of it all; I said, "It's a tubal pregnancy."

Mrs. Dollar simply wailed and flung herself on the sofa. Rolle Dollar was slower to comprehend.

But before either of them could start talking about funeral arrangements, I said, "No I want you to listen carefully to me. Mrs. Dollar, straighten up and pay attention!" Few people ever talked to her with that tone and she sat up and ceased her blubbering. "This condition has always been fatal, but it is now within the realm of the surgeon to correct. I know a surgeon in Cincinnati who has operated successfully and I want to take Angeline there. Right away. Rolle, you'll have to make immediate arrangements for a closed wagon. I want a litter suspended by leather straps to take up the shocks. In Austin we'll put her in a private car—this will cost a lot of money, but we're talking about the girl's life."

"I'll take care of it," Dollar said solemnly. He looked at his wife, then left the house. I rolled down my sleeves and slipped into my coat, trying to think of something to say. There wasn't anything.

Mrs. Dollar said, "Lunsford Cardine should be killed."

"Do you think that matters now? I have a

telegram to send. I'll be back this afternoon. We ought to be able to catch the night train out of Austin tomorrow evening and be in Cincinnati by early tomorrow afternoon. Try to get a grip on yourself now, Mrs. Dollar. Don't go to pieces on me."

"I'll try," she said. "Oh, what a cross to bear. What a curse!"

Rolle Dollar had the blacksmith build it to my instructions and I suppose that it was the first ambulance Victoria had ever seen. We took a spring wagon, made heavy top bows and erected wooden sides and covered them with canvas. Inside, the litter was suspended like a hammock and the patient would ride in relative comfort. Two jump seats were installed because both Christina Heidler and I intended to ride back there.

Quite a crowd gathered outside Rolle Dollar's house when we brought Angeline outside in a litter, swathed in blankets until only her head protruded. Rolle and another man hefted her into the ambulance; the luggage that Christina and I had brought along was stowed under the front seat and I went around to check it.

Guy Hulse sat on the seat and he grinned at me. "What the hell are you doing?" I said, surprised to see him.

"Why, I'm goin' to drive you to Austin, Doc.

Seen Rolle at the blacksmith shop and he told me you was takin' Angeline east, so I said I'd drive."

"You're a damned good man, Guy," I said and went back; Christina was inside and Aaron Stiles from the newspaper was there with his pad and pencil.

"Care to tell me anything, Doc?"

"Bad appendix," I said, loud enough so that others heard. "I know a surgeon in Cincinnati who operates successfully for that. We're taking her there."

"Serious as that, huh?" Stiles said, writing away.

"Fatal if not operated on," I said and got into the back and closed the doors. Suddenly Mrs. Dollar came bowling out of the house; I guess it just hit her that we were actually taking Angeline away and I rapped on the front window, telling Guy Hulse to get going.

It would be simple to say that we reached Austin without incident and an hour later got on the train, which is what we did, yet what happened bears telling.

Guy Hulse and his brother, Alfy, had been in town when they got word we were going to make a night drive of it to Austin, and Guy volunteered to drive while Alfy, on a fast horse, rode on ahead on a mission that was not clear to me until later, around ten o'clock to be exact.

The weather was cold and windy, but the tight

sides of the wagon helped hold it back. For a time I kept a kerosene lantern going, for heat more than light, but the fumes became strong and I had to put it out. Christina and I were bundled in heavy coats and mittens and we kept Angeline swathed in blankets, and I give her credit for having grit; she wasn't one for crying out in pain and I knew there was pain.

I could have given her a shot to ease the pain, but with the temperature near freezing, I felt it was better to wait until morning, until it warmed up a little.

Around ten o'clock I heard Guy Hulse whoa the team and stop and I opened the back door and got down to see what the trouble was. Some cowboys from the Rafter K outfit had built a huge fire alongside the road and they came around to the back with lanterns and torches. One toothless gnome of a man had a coffee pot and tin cups and another had a kettle of hot soup.

It was a thing that could almost bring tears to a man's eyes, and nothing tasted better. Christina Heidler spooned coffee and soup into Angeline Dollar and then some cowboys came to the back of the wagon, carrying hot rocks in their chap legs, using them like slings. They dumped the rocks into the back of the ambulance, at least a dozen headsized, and immediately the heat began to radiate.

They had heated them for four or five hours and

the heat would remain a long time. Up front, Guy Hulse and some of the Rafter K outfit hitched up a team of fresh horses and before I could express my thanks, we were moving again.

Now I could see what Alfy Hulse was doing, riding out a cold and blustery night, wearing out Lord knew how many horses, going ahead of us, telling whoever he met that we were on a mission of mercy.

By morning, I had hoped to reach Gonzales, but there was the river to cross and the freeze-thaw, see-saw kind of weather we'd been having would leave the river swollen and I expected trouble there.

There wasn't, really, because we were met by thirty riders from the T-On-A-Rail outfit. They'd spent hours cutting timber and roping together a raft and when we stopped, they had coffee and bacon and biscuits waiting for us, and another load of hot rocks.

The team was unhitched and the ambulance rolled onto the raft; it settled deeper into the water but the wheel rims did not get too wet. Then the cowboys made their ropes fast to the raft and to a man plunged their horses into the icy water and swam us across. A huge fire had been built up on the far bank; fresh horses were hitched and we moved on without delay.

Dawn brought a gray, cheerless sky, and with the inside of the ambulance kept reasonably warm by the rocks, I gave Angeline an injection and she slept.

At a stage station twenty miles south of Austin we ran into the first of the snow; it continued to snow from then on, light, drifting flakes, more powder than anything, but keeping up steadily it soon layered the land a brilliant white.

Alfy Hulse was at the stage station; he opened the back door and grinned at me as Christina and I stepped down. Alfy Hulse showed the effects of a sleepless night, and the hard riding.

The first thing he said was, "You all right, Doc? Everything all right?"

I shook hands with him, too moved to speak, then we went inside briefly. The station agent and two Mexican hostlers carried heated rocks in the tin coal scuttle and placed them inside the ambulance and before they closed the door, the Mexicans crossed themselves.

Sedated, Angeline would sleep so I felt no sense of guilt when I backed up to the stove alongside Christina and toasted some heat into my backside.

Alfy and Guy Hulse brought us some coffee. I looked from one to the other and said, "Rolle Dollar owes you more than he can ever repay. Are you both going on to Austin?" I expected that perhaps Alfy would stay at the station and wait for Guy to come back.

"We're goin' on," Guy said. "Angeline, she's

109

makin' it, ain't she, Doc?" He looked at his brother and shifted his feet. "Doc, I know a telegram costs money, but after the operation, I'd appreciate it if you'd wire us and let us know how it came out."

"Why," I said, "I'd be glad to do that." I studied them briefly. "Say, have you got a personal interest in Angeline, boys?"

Alfy shrugged. "She don't know we're alive, Doc. It don't matter none though."

I said, "But soft, what light thru yon window breaks? It is the east and Juliet is the sun."

"What's that mean?" Alfy asked.

I reached out both hands and encompassed two shoulders. "Boys, promise me one thing? When she comes home, comb your hair and bring her— well, don't bring her anything. Just come and see her!"

Alfy shook his head. "I don't know, Doc. Rolle Dollar's got some set ideas and he knows that both Guy and me ain't above havin' a drink now and then."

"Rolle Dollar will be a changed man, believe me." I took a notebook and pencil from my pocket and wrote for several minutes, then I gave the page to Guy Hulse. "Will you see that the telegrapher gets this in Austin?" I gave him five dollars to pay for it. "Read it if you want."

"Neither of us can read, Doc," Alfy said solemnly.

"Then I'll tell you what it says. I told Rolle what you two have done and what the men of the Rafter K and T-On-A-Rail have done. I suggested that he sit down at his desk, with pen in hand and humility in heart and write his letters of thanks."

"Aw," Guy said, "you didn't have to do that. The fellas were glad to do it."

What was there to say?

It was time to leave and we got into the ambulance. Alfy tied two fresh saddle horses on behind and we started off. I remained quiet, thinking about this night and how I probably would never forget any of it.

A man cannot practice medicine on the frontier without getting to know a lot of people, and in both the cow outfits I recognized men that were considered extremely dangerous by peace officers, some with pretty wide reputations as gunfighters and killers. In general they were an unwashed, profane lot, living dangerous, lonely lives and any of them would be lucky to live to the age of forty.

But that night, there were no kinder hearts, no gentler hands, no feeling more sincere than each of them felt. And every one of them knowing that they were helping a girl whose station was above them, unjustly, perhaps, but there nevertheless.

It was a cruel paradox that could anger a man a little.

Christina Heidler spoke. "I love you, Ted Bodry."

I looked at her in the pale light filtering through the front window. She took off her mitten and slipped her warm firm hand into my mitten and her fingers were strong.

"Dr. Ivy helped me because he's a doctor. You helped me because you're kind. It doesn't bother me to tell you that I love you. I can live with it because it will be enough."

———10

Dr. Harry Calendar met the train and I hardly recognized him, muffled so in a great fur coat. He had an ambulance waiting and Angeline Dollar was transferred immediately; Christina and I rode in Calendar's coach while hospital orderlies went in the ambulance.

The snow was deep, banked along the edges of the street and carriage wheels had been replaced by sled runners. Calendar produced a lap robe for our feet and on the way to the hospital I discussed Angeline's case with him. As I expected, he intended to operate immediately and he wanted me to assist, but I had to decline. I wanted to observe closely his technique before I was prepared to assist.

And he understood.

He had taken rooms for us in a small hotel three

blocks from the hospital; we had only to register and get our key from the desk clerk. He was the same Harry Calendar, always in command, always thinking of everything.

At the hospital we separated and Harry gave us instructions as to how to get to the surgical amphitheater. We walked down several long halls and found a gathering by a large double door. On the wall was a notice board, with a list of operations and surgeons scheduled; it rather boggled me, that more surgery was being performed in one day than I would do in six months.

We went in and took seats; they encircled the operating room, sharply tiered so that those observing got an unobstructed view directly over the operating table. There was, for me, a great excitement that I had not felt since my medical school days and I had forgotten how many were in attendance on the patient. Dr. Calendar was assisted by two surgeons, and there was a scrub nurse, a surgical nurse, and two nurses administering the anaesthetic. I was particularly interested in the equipment for spraying the instruments with antiseptics (boiling had not yet come into practice; I suppose it was so simple no one ever thought of it).

I was impressed with the way the surgical nurse prepared the patient, first carefully washing and shaving the area to be incised. Later I learned that this was becoming more accepted as a method of introducing better sepsis; the minute hair follicles can hide bacteria and the policy of shaving pubic hair during normal delivery was encouraged in the better hospitals.

The first incision interested me because a dye was used to trace the exact location of the incision before any instrument was introduced. Abdominal entry had always concerned me because the abdominal wall contains important nerves and muscles and the surgeon cannot simply hack his way through them; the incision has to be made in such a way as to do the minimum of harm.

Dr. Calendar made his first incision some three inches long in a downward and inward slope, cutting between the muscles rather than across them and I was interested to note that his single cut was through the sheath of the main muscle, the rectus abdominis, one stroke, not a series of deeper cuts which always left the opening a bit ragged.

For thirty-seven minutes I watched, never once taking my eyes off his hands and it is difficult to say how I really felt about it all. He was like a grand musician playing a silent, magnificent organ, deft, certain, incredibly delicate. Without discussing the matter with him, I assumed that the operation would terminate in a complete hysterectomy, dangerous, with high mortality; I could have foreseen no other course.

And I could not have been more mistaken.

With a technique certainly advanced he meticulously closed, suturing carefully, minutely, and when he had finished and stripped off his gown, I left with Christina Heidler, feeling quite drained. We waited for him in the hallway and after a few minutes he came out, shrugging into his coat. He was a thick-set man, rather short, with rich dark hair and he wore gold-rimmed glasses. In age he was close to thirty and certainly already established in surgical fields.

We went into a cafeteria in the basement of the hospital and took a corner table. Harry Calendar said, "Prognosis, good, Doctor. She should convalesce here for at least a month before making that long journey back. Traveling such distances alone—"

"Maybe we can work something out, Harry. I would like to have Miss Heidler remain here for some nurse's training, particularly in surgery." He looked at her. "If you don't mind, Christina, you could return with her."

"An excellent arrangement," Calendar said. Then he winked. "You've got a damned pretty nurse, Doctor. Trade you."

"Thank you, no," I said. "But speaking of nurses, I was really impressed with your surgical assistants. I've always felt that I never had enough hands, Harry, and now I see that it's nearly impossible for a man to do competent surgery without proper assistance."

"Surgery is undergoing a tremendous upheaval," Calendar said. "For centuries it has been the by-product of medicine, almost sheer butchery. But of course anesthesia has removed the horror of it to a large degree and people no longer hold surgical practice in dread. Well, at least they are becoming educated to it. And surgery is just not suited to home laying-in, Ted. The patient must be hospitalized and postoperative care is often as important as the surgical procedure itself. When I went into residency here three years ago, the surgical facilities were rather inconsequential. I would say that they have expanded to ten times what they were then and plans are under advisement for building another wing." He took a slim cigar from his pocket, offered one to me, then lit both of them. "Are you still in practice with Dr. Walter Ivy?" I nodded. "Quite a fellow there. Very good, I understand. Tremendous bedside manner."

"I take it you don't approve."

Harry Calendar shrugged. "Ted, you just don't have the knack for telling a joke, passing on gossip, and handing the patient a pill. I detected that right away while you were a student. You were very intense. Very questioning. It takes that to be a surgeon."

"Well, I certainly feel inadequate enough," I admitted. "That's why I snapped at the chance to come back for a few weeks. I intend to spend a good deal of my time in the amphitheater taking profuse notes."

Calendar laughed. "There'll be ample opportunity, Ted, because we have some men here who are doing very advanced work, particularly in vermiform appendix disease, or typhlitis or perityphlitis, or whatever you happen to want to call it. These abdominal infections are often terminal and there's considerable research to determine cause and arrest."

"Yes, I lost four patients of typhlitis. As a matter of fact, I suspected that in the Dollar girl."

"It's none of my business," Harry Calendar said, "but her husband didn't come along?"

I glanced at Christina, then said, "He's, ah—"

"Of course," Calendar said, assuming the obvious. "I should have known. Well, it's a shame because the odds are that she could conceive again, normally." He drew deeply on his cigar. "We've got a man here from Vienna who's doing some interesting hernia work. He's just published an important paper on the removal of a cancerous larynx, but his real devotion is to gastric surgery. He's operating twice this week and once the next. You'll want to observe."

"I certainly will!"

Harry Calendar looked at his watch. "I'm due on the wards. Why don't you go to your hotel and rest up. I'll meet you in the dining room at seven and we'll have dinner. If possible, I'll bring along a man you'll find very interesting. He's doing some new work on kidney stones." He got up and smiled at Christina. "Beautiful, simply beautiful, Doctor."

Then he hurried off; he never seemed to walk anywhere.

I looked at Christina and she was looking at me; we both laughed.

"He's an unusual man," I said.

"Oh, but *very* interesting," she said, in that way women use that arouses an instant jealousy.

The hospital had a training program for nurses and Christina Heidler attended these daily, beginning early in the morning and not terminating until late evening and I would see her only at dinner and perhaps a hour or so afterward.

I was very busy, attending lectures, observing surgical technique, and digging into the business of operating a hospital because I intended to have one of my own; there was no doubt in my mind that the administrative work would fall to me and not be shared by Walter Ivy who was always very busy being the good country doctor.

Angeline Dollar was in the surgical ward and I paid a visit each day; after all, she was still my patient and her recovery was steady, each day releasing her a bit from pain, and finally on the tenth day she was allowed to walk around a bit, supported by two nurses. Of course today we get the surgical patient right out of bed and make them go to the bathroom, but then we believed in strict rest and quiet, and actually retarded their recovery.

It seemed inconceivable that my visit was at an end; the time had gone so rapidly. Since I had to catch a ten o'clock train, Harry Calendar dined with Christina and me in my hotel room, and professing a call, he left early.

Of course I wanted to be alone with her, and I said all the stupid things men say, like, "Are you sure you'll be all right? Do you have enough money? You will wire me so I can meet your train?"

None of it was any good, because I had once acted as though I couldn't love her and now I sat there like an oaf, actually in love with her and not knowing at all how the devil to say it.

It was a dismal situation.

Then she said, "You're not very good at small talk, are you, Ted?"

"Abominable."

"Then why try?"

"It's been a full, exciting ten days, hasn't it?" I fell quiet, brushing lightly at my mustache. "You know, Harry's right; you're a lovely girl. I've always thought so." Again that blasted silence. Finally I flung out of the chair and moved to her and pulled her to her feet. "In the name of God,

Christina, marry me and settle once and for all this infernal ache inside me!"

"You only have an hour before train time," she reminded me.

"Blast the train! You're not being very romantic, you know."

She put her soft hands on my face and kissed me lightly. "Ted, go home. Think about it. When I come back you'll know if you really want that."

"Damn it, I know now!"

"No, you think about it. Please?"

"You're bound to get your way," I said. "All right, Christina, I'll go and I'll think about it but I won't change my mind."

"It's hard to tell these things, Ted. But if you do, I'll understand. Honestly."

I still had my hands on her arms and I gently drew her to me; she came willingly and I held her while I kissed her; it was the most satisfying experience of my life.

She wanted to go with me to the train but I wouldn't hear of it; it was almost zero out and I knew she had to get up early the next morning. So we didn't say goodbye; I just left with my bags, caught a carriage and arrived at the station just in time to get aboard.

Although it was more expensive, I had a compartment to myself and spent the long hours studying and recompiling my volumes of notes.

At Austin there was a half a day lay over before I could catch the southbound coach; the weather was cold and windy and I wasn't looking forward to the stage ride.

Walter Ivy met me at the hotel and the weather was as balmy as a spring day, with a warming wind coming in off the gulf. He helped me with my luggage and bales of books and notes, then said, "How's your patient?"

"Recovering. Would you mind dropping me off at the Dollar house?"

"They got your wire. Can't it wait?" He saw that it couldn't and sighed and clucked to the team. When I got out of the buggy by Rolle Dollar's gate, Walter said, "I'll unload this stuff for you. Why don't you have supper with us?"

"Are you sure Dorsey won't mind?"

He smiled. "She's settled down in her pregnancy, and is feeling much better." He popped the lid on his watch. "Say an hour?"

I nodded and he drove on.

When I turned up the path, Rolle Dollar came to the front door and held it open for me. He seized my hand and nearly broke my knuckles. "Mrs. Dollar is in her room; I'll fetch her. Make yourself at home, Doctor."

I sat down and she came in a moment later; Rolle had his arm around her and this display of affection surprised me. Mrs. Dollar wanted to shake my hand and she screwed up her face as though on the verge of tears but managed by supreme control not to cry.

Rolle said, "We got your wire. The first one, and the last one that you sent after the operation. It humbles a man. Indeed it does." He looked genuinely sorry. "I sat up all that night, reading the Word, and taking stock of myself, Doctor. I've cast many a stone at the Hulse brothers and at old Pete. Shiftless, I've called them. And worse too. Not fit, I've said." He sniffed. "I went to 'em. Yessir, I did that. I went a humble man. They took me into their house, such as it is, gave me food and drink and we talked as friends. That Alfy is a straight-forward boy, that he is. Unlettered, to be sure, but straight in the eye and heart. And that's what matters, isn't it?"

"It's a pretty good world, Rolle. A little rough around the edges, but a good world. Your daughter will regain her health. Someday she'll marry and, well, she may even make you a grandfather."

"Praise God," Rolle said.

"Amen," said his wife.

He cleared his throat. "You know I hold drink to be one of man's greatest sins, Doctor, but I ordered two cases of the best whiskey from Mulligan and sent a case to the men at the Rafter T and a case to T-On-A-Rail."

"You did the right thing, Rolle. It was something they'll understand and remember."

He nodded, feeling a little better about it, I suppose. Then he said, "I'd like to know that doctor's fee. Send him a check first thing in the morning."

I reached inside my coat. "I brought the bill, Rolle. With hospital care and surgeon's fees, it comes to two hundred and eight dollars."

He took the bill from me, not batting an eye, and this from a man who had fifty cents of the first dollar he ever earned.

"I expect you've got a bill for me."

"I'll tell you what, Rolle. You have an ambulance built for me to my specifications and I'll call it square. Cut any corners you want, but I mean to have a carriage that a person in pain can ride in without jolting their insides loose."

"By the Lord in Heaven," Rolle Dollar said, "you'll have it!"

——11

Generally, when people say they'll do something it means when they get around to it, or in their own sweet time, so I was a little surprised when a week later, Rolle Dollar approached my table at the hotel and sat down across from me. He eyed my pushed-aside plate, the remaining pie crumbs and my almost finished cup of coffee.

"About through there, Doc?"

"Except for a cigar and the expulsion of a little swallowed air."

"I want you to come down to Peerly's blacksmith shop."

"Now?"

He bobbed his head, so I laid fifty cents on the table, gathered up hat, coat, and bag and went out with him, putting them on as we went through the lobby.

We walked two blocks down and Rolle seemed almost on the verge of trotting ahead of me, he was that excited. He opened the door for me and I stepped inside the shop. Peerly's blacksmith shop was dirty; they all were, with a profusion of iron scattered about and horseshoes hanging from the rafters and the place was cozy from the forge fire. Rolle led the way back; Peerly was there, whistling away and we stepped through another door. There were lanterns hanging from the uprights and I stopped just inside the door, like a man will when his breath is a bit taken away.

Rolle Dollar rocked back and forth on his heels. "How do you like it, Doc?"

He meant my ambulance. My beautiful ambulance. I walked around it examining it while Amos Peerly and Rolle Dollar stood there, pleased with it all. Peerly had taken a stage coach running gear and overhauled it; it was painted black with gilt striping, a gleaming, immaculate thing. And on this chassis he had constructed an ambulance body of solid oak with double doors in the back; the whole thing was suspended by broad leather straps which would give it the easy, rocking chair ride of a stage. The body was painted a glistening white and the driver sat outside, forward, on a high perch. Inside there was a suspended litter and two upholstered jump seats. A storm lantern had been fastened to the roof and, outside, two large coach lights with polished reflectors would brighten any dark avenue.

I went over to where they waited and waved my hands, wondering what I could say. "Rolle, I want the Hulse boys to take this to Austin to meet the train. We'll bring Angeline home in it."

"That's mighty nice, Doc, but I told Alfy Hulse he could use my buggy. It's kinda that I want to see my little girl sittin' up."

"Sure," I said. "That'll do fine, Rolle." Then I looked at Amos Peerly. "How long have you been workin' on this, Amos?"

"I got started the day after you got back, Doc. Ain't done nothin' else, really." He grinned. "But I enjoyed every minute of it. Even the undertaker ain't got a rig this fancy." He took me forward, towing me by the arm and showed me what he'd built under the front seat. It was a heavy metal box with a drawer that pulled forward. "You just fill this with coals on a cold night and the heat goes into the back to take the chill off. Ought to make it cozy as a kitchen, Doc."

It was ingenious and I examined it in detail with the flue that carried the heated air into the back without introducing fumes. The fire box was surrounded by an air chamber which vented under the seat.

"It's the best coach I've ever seen, Amos!"

"Never built anything like it before," Peerly admitted. "Always wanted to build coaches. Started out that way back east, then I came here and took up blacksmithing."

"Tomorrow morning I'll drive it up and down the street so everybody can see it." We went back into the blacksmith shop. "Rolle, Amos, I thank you and a lot of people will thank you."

Peerly waved his hand and Rolle Dollar said, "Doc, I just want to see my little girl step out of that buggy under her own steam and smile. She's all the missus and I've got. Comes down to it, nothin' else really matters."

Alfy and Guy Hulse came to see me before they left for Austin; they wanted to know if there was anything special they had to do, and I suggested that they make sure they had an extra lap robe and didn't try to make sixty miles a day. They grinned at this and poked each other on the arm and left my office.

I could understand their impatience; I was

impatient myself, but not to have Angeline Dollar back. The last ten days had been lonesome ones for me, making my rounds and returning to an empty office.

It is still amazing to me how men can develop a specific blindness when it concerns a woman. From the first I had wanted Christina Heidler to stay, telling myself that she needed a place of her own, and I think I really believed that. And subsequently I encouraged her to remain, tying her, really, hoping she would become so dependent that she would dare not leave me; I suppose I had that subconscious fear that she would leave. And all the time I was talking one thing and feeling another.

A miserable situation for a professional man, and one I didn't enjoy.

As much time as possible was spent west of town where a crew of twenty workmen, mostly Mexican, were laboring to complete the foundations. The concrete had been hauled in from Port Lavaca and after fifteen days of forming, the basement and walls were finally poured.

Had the details been left to me I would have made a lot of mistakes and spent money needlessly; we were spared this through the efforts of Leland Burgess, the attorney from San Antonio. He had duplicates made of the plans and contractors were invited to submit bids, with the upshot being that a local firm would build the foundation, an Austin company would erect walls and structure, while a San Antonio company would install all plumbing and heating. Well drilling was done locally and a New England firm shipped the first windmill in south Texas; this unit pumped the water into a huge storage tank, highly elevated, and from there the water was piped throughout the building.

Indoor plumbing, novelty though it was, had finally come west.

Completion date was scheduled for early fall of 1874, and then, with the building up, work would only begin for me, since the organization and administration were going to be my responsibility.

Walter Ivy and I spent three days out of town; we had a few outlying towns where we held clinics. This was Walter's idea and we had been doing it for some time, generally alternating office and home calls. He had set up a schedule so that we always arrived at the same time of the month and set up in a small place reserved for us. Each month we would make the rounds, stopping at two large ranches to the southwest, a small village populated mainly by Mexicans, and ending with a swing north that brought us back to Victoria.

And it seemed to me that people saved up all their aches and pains for our monthly visits. We worked together at the ranches and Walter remained there while I made a tour to some of the places owned by homesteaders; they would leave a message for me, saying they were feeling poorly or that this was bothering them, or something. Always something.

And I noticed that during this last year more and more homesteaders were nibbling away at the lands preempted by the big ranches. Fences were going up and the plowed field was becoming more commonplace. Orchards were planted and wheat was being sown and cotton fields sprang up and the face of Texas was slowly, surely being changed.

The temper of Texas was changing too for I noticed that the cowboys all wore their pistols, even around the ranch house, and that talk was going around about fence cutting and pretty soon we'd have the Texas Rangers if the cattlemen didn't put away their snippers.

Homesteaders were watching carefully anyone who came near their places and there was not one house that I was able to approach without being covered by a rifle or shotgun. Weapons were only put away after I was identified.

On the way back Walter and I talked about this; he had a nose for trouble and suspected that pretty soon we'd be getting a rash of gunshot cases, and he figured it was only a matter of time before the law stepped in.

I suppose it was my youth, but I was more confident in the sound judgment of man, then I remembered the senseless shooting in Mulligan's place and didn't shrug off his opinion too lightly. After all, few men had the feel of the country like Walter Ivy had; he seemed to have a finger eternally on the pulse. And he knew these people, understood them better than I did, perhaps better than I ever would. Where I lost patience with them, he maintained his. Where I considered them backward, he thought of them as conservative. I thought they were too provincial; he felt that they were just set in their ways.

It was, I'm sure, this genuine compassion that made Walter Ivy so popular and influential. In the many meetings I had attended with him—the town council and the school board—I have watched him sit there, slumped in his chair, littering the front of his vest with fingernail scrapings, apparently removed from mounting arguments. Then he would clear his throat and everyone would stop talking and he'd sit there, his eyebrows bunched up, and put his knife away. When he stood up, everyone listened to him and I would hesitate to say how many foolish moves this procedure has halted.

It brought us a fire department, and a public park, and two new churches and a two storey school house, the only one south of Austin.

Many of Walter Ivy's medical views did not

coincide with mine, but that he was a sensible man with both feet firmly rooted in Texas soil was beyond dispute; he seemed determined to do what was best for the most people and because of this he would have made a poor politician.

We arrived home late, as usual. Dorsey had retired and I was ready to collapse, but I heated water for a bath, soaked weariness away, then had a stiff drink of whiskey and went to bed.

The sun coming through my window woke me and I shaved before bundling into my coat and going uptown. It was early, but I wanted to be early; this was the day the Hulse brothers should be coming back.

Rolle Dollar and his wife were at the hotel and there was a goodly crowd around, waiting for the ambulance to show up. My intentions had a short life when one of Ben Titus' deputies came up to me and drew me aside. "Hate to spoil this home-comin', Doc, but I do wish you'd come over to the jail and have a look at Ben. We just can't seem to wake him at all."

All this was done quietly; no one else had heard him. I said, "All right, I'll go right over. But get Dr. Ivy too."

"Sure thing." He trotted off down the street and I unhurriedly left the hotel and walked a block and a half over to the jail. The other deputy was with Ben Titus; he was in the spare room where he slept when he was on duty.

Obviously he had gone to bed in a normal manner, or normal for a lawman; boots and gun off. His breathing was shallow and his pulse was extremely faint. I examined his eyes and had just about decided when Walter Ivy came in, quite out of breath.

"I think it's his heart," I said, stepping back so that Walter could attend him. Finally he motioned for me to help him remove Ben's shirt and vest and roll the sleeve of his underwear; I took out my knife and slit it to the shoulder and Walter prepared an injection.

He motioned for me to check his pulse and I did while he slowly pressed the plunger. Within seconds it seemed that Ben's pulse grew stronger and we watched him closely for a half hour. By then Walter was satisfied that Titus was resting easy.

"I don't think he dare be moved, Ted," Walter said gravely. He looked at the deputies; the other one had come in earlier but I hadn't noticed. "He's got a bad heart and he needs complete rest and quiet."

"Is he goin' to be all right, Doc?"

Walter looked at the man, then said, "I honestly don't know. I would say for certain that if he recovers, it'll mean taking things very easy for the rest of his life."

The two deputies looked at each other, the question in their eyes. "We got to get a new sheriff, huh?" One scrubbed the back of his neck with his hands. "I don't want the job, Doc. You, Herbie?"

Herbie shook his head, and Walter Ivy said, "Ted, stay here. I'll go see Aaron Stiles and Butram Cardine. I'll try not to be long."

I understood what he had to do for the mechanics of government had to go on and someone would have to be appointed sheriff until next election. And I believed him when he said he'd try not to be long, but I really wished he'd stayed in attendance and let me go back to the main street.

But I stayed and missed out on it all; Ivy was gone almost two hours and when he did come back I had to work at controlling my temper. And he knew it because he said, "I really am sorry, Ted."

"Forget it, Walter."

"I really am—"

"The patient comes first," I said. "Are you going to stay here now?"

"Yes, for a while." Then he smiled. "That was a pretty sight, that ambulance. I'd get over to your office right away, if I was you." Then he took my sleeve. "Ted, are you going to marry her?"

"If she'll have me."

He thought about it. "She's a strong woman, boy. She won't tame into a lap cat."

"Who wants one?" I said and went out, hurrying now.

I stopped in my office just long enough to fling my bag on the couch, then went through my room to the short hallway connecting the storeroom and Christina's.

Before I knocked I heard her moving about, then I heard her voice and opened the door. She had her luggage on the bed and was putting things away and when I stepped into the room she put the things down and watched me.

"Ben Titus had a heart attack and I had—"

The devil with the explanations. I went to her and put my arms around her and kissed her and she came full against me, warm and yielding and then she put her head against my shoulder and rested there.

"I told you it wouldn't matter if you'd changed your mind," she said softly. "But it did. When you weren't there—"

"I wanted to be, Christina. I tried to be. But damn it all—"

"It's all right now," she said and laughed and pulled away from me. "Everything's all right now."

"And our patient?"

"Well. She stood the trip nicely."

I took her arm and brought her to me again; it was maddening to have her so near and yet not close enough. "Tomorrow morning I'm going to the courthouse and take out a license. And in the afternoon we'll hitch up my buggy and see if we can't find a house for rent. I've missed you."

"It's been a long winter," she said softly. "But good."

I pulled my head back and looked at her. "Now what does that mean?"

She smiled. "It means I've waited a long time for you to put your arms around me, a long time for you to know that you could love me." She sighed and rested her head against me. "Ted, I will spend my life trying to make you happy."

—12

Christina Heidler and I were married on Sunday, January 4, 1874, and Walter Ivy handled all the arrangements, renting the whole dining room of the hotel for the ceremony and I was quite stiff and nervous through the reception afterward. Reverend Loch Angevine performed the whole thing. Dorsey attended the ceremony and the reception, which surprised me because this was the first time she had left her house since she arrived. She was heavy with child and short of breath and Walter was very attentive, but then I suspect that he always had been.

I felt sure that things weren't going right between them although he never said anything and I didn't expect him to because he was a man who kept his personal business to himself. And Dorsey was not the wife he had expected or hoped for but Walter had made his bargain and would stick to it; he was that kind of a man. It must have been very difficult for a young woman, accustomed to servants and plenty of money and the comforts of a large eastern city to adjust to life in a Texas town. She surely must have missed the gay social life, but more I think she missed the gentle, mature surroundings of Maryland. Texas was a place of extremes. Even the weather was that way, hot as blazes or cold as the Klondike. Surely there was no one in town who was her equal, culturally, and she had made no friends at all. I'm sure ladies tried to call on her, and knowing Dorsey, I'm equally sure she rebuffed them.

And in Texas you only do that once.

Dorsey would never have admitted it, but she was a snob. In Baltimore, where the industrial climate was largely manufacturing, she circulated in a circle of mill owners and plant owners; I don't think she ever talked to a sweaty Polish worker or spoke to a tobacco-chewing Swede, or listened to the troubles of an Irish immigrant.

But in Victoria, Texas, she couldn't ignore the cowboys and cattle and rough men and rough country; it was always there, out her window, every time she looked. In the summer, dust settled over everything and a house was nigh impossible to keep clean; she must have fretted endlessly over this. Men swore and ladies pretended not to hear it and there was always the flavor of the cattle yard east of town when the wind was right, and it was, most of the time.

She was a very unhappy, very pregnant woman, and it was my thought that she wished there was some way to undo the whole thing.

However, I wasn't going to worry about Dorsey.

Christina and I had planned to go to Austin for ten days on our honeymoon; we intended to leave on the morning stage and I had my suitcases all packed. Our house wouldn't be vacant until then and we were going to stay the night in the hotel, and leave about ten in the morning.

I had considered all arrangements made, finalized, and finished.

But you never can tell.

Christina was the center of all attention and Walter Ivy took my arm and drew me out of the lobby to a small pantry off the kitchen. His manner was grave and he kept running his hands through his thinning hair. "Ted, I'm afraid something's come up that involves you. Wish to God it didn't, but it does and I can't help it." He looked at me steadily and I could see that it was an effort. "Dorsey has made up her mind to go back home, Ted." He nodded. "Yes, she's going to leave in the morning. It's been coming. I knew it but hoped that somehow—" He shrugged the rest of that away. "The thing is, Ted, I love that woman. Worship the ground she walks on. I'm going with her, Ted. What else can I do?"

I can't say that I was surprised, but I was shocked that it would happen at such an inopportune time. "Walter, don't give in to her! It's the worst thing you could do."

"I know it but I can't help myself."

"What about your practice here?"

"Give it up, I guess. I'd like to see you buy it, Ted."

"I can't. All my money is tied up in the hospital. And what about yours, Walter?"

"Have to withdraw it," he said.

I could feel my temper rising and not at the predicament this placed me in, but at Dorsey for doing this. "Walter, you know I can't refuse, but get Dorsey and meet me upstairs in my room. Thirty-one at the near end of the hall."

Before he could object I left him and went up the stairs. I paced a bit and lit a cigar and then Walter knocked and opened the door for Dorsey. I could see by her expression that she was plenty put out about this, so I came right to the point. "Dorsey, I understand you're going home in the morning."

"Then you understand correctly," she said. "What of it?"

"Frankly," I said, "I don't care where you go,

but since Walter is going with you, I have to take over his practice and we have to reach some kind of terms."

"Practice?" she said, making it into a dirty word. "You call that a practice? I want him to go back to where he can be a *real* doctor. Why he could make fifteen thousand a year in Baltimore without ever leaving his office."

"Dorsey, I'm not interested in your greed. It's of no interest to me that you're a willful snob. Texas doesn't need you. You don't have anything they want."

"Now just a minute—" Walter began, but closed his mouth when I stared at him.

"No, you listen to me! I know everything I am is due to you and I'm not forgetting that. But this isn't the time to think of you or me. I'm thinking of our patients, the people who look to us for the only help they're going to get. You want me to buy you out and you know the only way I could do that is to give up the hospital. It might be six or eight years before I could begin building again. How many people will die in the mean-time because I wouldn't have the facilities to help them?"

"You're being ridiculous and dramatic," Dorsey said and I whirled on her.

"You shut your mouth! Since you've made no contribution, keep out of it." I looked at Walter Ivy. "This is what we're going to do, Walter.

You'll pull out of the hospital; that's four thousand. But you sign a quitclaim deed to your house. I'll turn *that* into a hospital until the other one is completed. At that time I'll put the house on the market and sell it for at least what it cost you to build it, plus an amount that would be reasonable rent for the time I've used it."

"Don't you do it, Walter!"

But he wasn't listening to her; he nodded and said, "All right, Ted. I'll have the papers in order by evening." He took Dorsey by the arm and steered her to the door and she balked because she had something to say to me.

"Oh, you're a snot, Ted. You've milked Walter for all you're going to. It's over! The ride on the man's back is over. You won't last by yourself because you need Walter to stand up. And when you fall, I'll laugh!"

"Come along, Dorsey." He tugged at her arm and pulled her into the hall and found Christina standing there.

Dorsey stared at her and said, "Don't think a wedding ring changes anything for you." Then she started to cry uncontrollably and Walter Ivy shook his head and led her sobbing down the hall.

After they disappeared down the stairs, Christina came inside and I closed the door. She said, "Dorsey is so unhappy that she hates everything. She didn't mean a thing she said."

"You're a lovely bride," I said.

She smiled and took off her veil and carefully put it on the dresser. "I think I know what's the matter with Dorsey. For the first time in her life she doubts that she is woman enough for Walter, or woman enough to live here. All around her she sees people whom she always considered inferior and now she understands that here they are better than she is. It's a hard thing to know."

"We're not going to be able to go on a honeymoon, Mrs. Bodry."

She smiled and tilted her head to one side. "I have a feeling that it won't matter."

And then she came to me, my arms went around her, and I was pretty sure that she was right.

I'm not sure that I really became accustomed to having Walter Ivy gone; certainly it meant a heavier burden for me and there were days on end when I got up at sunrise and didn't sit down with my wife and have supper until ten o'clock at night.

Many of Walter's civic duties fell to me and I tried to dispatch them with the thoughtful attention that Walter had always given them. With Ben Titus recovering from his heart attack, the county supervisors asked my recommendation for sheriff, until next election. At that time and place, honesty and courage were attributes more important than education and knowledge of law, and I suggested Alfy Hulse. He was only twenty-four, but his reputation was well established and he had the respect of all who knew him.

He was sworn in in mid-February and it was a proud day for Old Pete.

Work continued on the hospital, with Rolle Dollar and Butram Cardine coming up with the money that Walter Ivy had withdrawn.

Spring came early with warming winds and a good sun and I noticed that new people were coming to town, some in wagons, and some on the stage. A land office opened up on main street and business took a turn upward and I noticed that Miller's store was stocking new items.

Rolle Dollar told me that his hardware business was growing for these farmers had money, and even though a lot of them were Yankees, they got along well, went quietly about their business, joined the churches and sent their children to school.

In May, I got a letter from Walter Ivy; he was in practice in Baltimore and Dorsey had had her baby, a boy. She seemed, according to Walter, quite happy now and spent a good deal of her time with her family. But a letter is many things; it is the words written and the words implied and judged against prior knowledge of the writer, it reveals things unspoken.

Walter's practice was substantially better paying than what he had in Victoria for he largely served only those who had money and he gave only a half day a week at the county hospital where the poor and the foreign-born went. He tried to convince me that he was happy and pleased, but I knew that he wasn't. Some doctors are content with token medicine while others are destined only to heal and suffer and die a little with each patient whose condition is terminal. I'd always known that Walter was that way. He'd doctor anyone, Mexican, Indian, poor, rich, anyone, and the money was the least of his worries, although he'd always made out that it meant a great deal to him.

But his words had never matched his deeds, and the deeds were what I judged him by.

He did not want me to write to him at his home and from that I gathered that Dorsey really held a grudge, so I wrote to him at his office and told him about Texas and the people he knew and how things were growing. And even as I did it I knew that it would get to him good because the man had roots here and even his wife couldn't tear them up.

I also wrote to several doctors, asking them whether or not they would be interested in coming to Victoria to establish themselves in my practice; my work load was getting very heavy and I knew that if it continued, I wouldn't be able to go it alone.

Christina was a tremendous help; she managed

as high as eight bed patients at a time for we had converted half of Walter's house to additional hospital space. And my reputation as a surgeon was spreading so that by summer time I had operated on and discharged sixteen patients who had traveled quite a distance for help.

I also lost four and this depressed me although I knew it had to happen occasionally.

The feelings between cattlemen and home-steaders began to take on an explosive potential around June because the creeks were down and the cattlemen always reached for all the grazing land they could get, fattening up for the fall market, and of course the farmers had their fences up and their crops coming up and threats passed back and forth.

An Ohio man named Will Stang was the leader of the farmer element; he was a nice man, medium height, with a slow way of talking and a lot of sense to what he said.

Stang had a Mexican boy working for him and one day—no one is sure just what set it off—the Mexican boy hauled off and knocked down one of the Circle B riders, and by the time the cowboy hit the dirt he had his six-shooter out and had put a ball right in the middle of the Mexican's chest.

By the time I was notified and got uptown, a huge crowd ringed the downed man and the priest was there, holding up his right hand and even as I knelt to make my examination I could hear him:

"Si vivis, ego te absolvo a peccatis tuis. In nomine Patris et Filii et Spiritus Sancti. Amen."

Then the Mexican boy died with my finger on his pulse and I looked at the priest and at the cowboy who stood there, still holding his six-shooter; blood dripped from a split lip but he paid no attention to it.

The priest said, "He is gone?"

I nodded and he bent and took a small vial of holy oil from his pocket and put some on his thumb and made a cross on the dead man's forehead. Then he stood up and went through the crowd and they gave way for him.

Alfy Hulse pushed through, took it all in at a glance, then held out his hand. "I'll take that pistol, Scotty. Let's have no more trouble now."

The cowboy flipped it around and handed it over butt first. Hulse put it in his hip pocket and took the cowboy by the arm. "I'll have to lock you up, Scotty." The cowboy nodded and went with him, offering no resistance.

Three weeks later, after Alfy Hulse had investi-gated and the grand jury convened, Scott Breedon was bound over for trial.

It seemed like everyone turned out for it and the courtroom wasn't nearly big enough to hold a fifth of the crowd, so they lined up to the bar at Mulligan's and across the street at the hotel and waited it out, the cattlemen on one side and the farmers on the other.

And in all of it, Buford Brittles remained neutral. His cowboys always came to town unarmed or if they felt they could not, they were fired and hired on somewhere else. Scully Beachamp did not go this far, but he would not side with the other ranchers and join their fence cutting and trouble making. Brittles and Beachamp waited out the trial on the hotel porch, which was the unspoken domain of the farmers. Will Stang was there and he talked to Brittles and Beachamp; I don't know what about.

When the jury came in, I was on call and didn't hear about it until that evening when I sat down to my supper. Christina gave me the news.

"The cowboy was fined five hundred dollars and put in jail for ninety days," she said. "It was pretty well established that the Mexican boy went out of his way to pick the fight."

"That's what I understand. It seems that he followed Scott Breedon from store to store, ragging him on." I sighed and sliced my roast beef. "Well, I'm sure it hasn't ended with the trial."

—13

The most uneasy kind of peace settled over the county because Alfy Hulse, in an unprecedented move, had Judge Enright place the principals under a three hundred dollar peace bond, and that just about included every cattleman and farmer within a radius of fifty miles. It looked like voter registration day at the courthouse and they stood in silent knots, faction against faction, waiting to pay the county clerk.

Now no one wanted to start the trouble, lose the money, and go to jail on top of it.

The hospital was becoming an imposing building, bright brick; the walls were up and the roof was being tiled and workers were busy completing the interior details. Daily I spent some time there, looking it over and as equipment arrived, I saw that it was stored properly and not tampered with.

Dr. Calendar recommended to me a young man who wanted to practice somewhere in the west; we exchanged letters and he sent references and he was scheduled to arrive in July. I had been in contact with three other men, all recommended highly by Walter J. Ivy; they were asked to leave their practices as soon as possible.

All these matters I discussed thoroughly with Buford Brittles and Scully Beachamp and Butram Cardine, who, at my insistence, sat as the hospital board on non-medical matters, and all funds were spent on a voucher over their signature. This, I felt, was business-like and promoted good faith in all concerned.

They were not partners, for after Walter pulled out I became the sole owner and the money advanced was a loan, on which interest would be paid and the principal amortized. My arrangements with the doctors were simple; they were in private practice at a central location, paying the hospital rent for their offices and using the hospital nursing staff.

Correspondence was a detail mercifully lifted from me by Christina, who wrote endless letters and inserted advertisements in many papers, including some in the eastern papers. Nursing, in those days, was really not a profession, at least in the United States, although Saint Thomas Hospital in London, England, turned out the finest nurses under the direction of Florence Nightingale.

All this correspondence resulted in the employment of six nurses, all trained to gently tend the sick, and they were to arrive in the early fall.

Two events occurred that I thought were of far-reaching effect; the Texas Rangers sent three men to Victoria to look into the fence cutting, which still continued in spite of the peace bond, and the Texas-Pacific Railroad was building trunk lines through Victoria to Port Lavaca.

To me this meant quicker, more reliable transportation and reconfirmed my belief that people would travel for many miles to undergo hospitalization and treatment. It also meant that I would get medical supplies from the east more quickly than by the present method of boat. Overland through the Indian country had never been good.

The army under MacKenzie was doing a job of keeping the Comanches and Kiowas contained in the central and north part of the state and we were enjoying some freedom from hostile raids, but no one was foolish enough to think this situation was permanent. There had always been times of peace, only to have it erupt into periods of intense fighting.

It just wasn't possible to convince a Texan that there was such a thing as a good, living Indian.

A social highlight occurred when Alfy Hulse and Angeline Dollar got married and Mrs. Dollar cried uncontrollably all through the ceremony. I suppose it was because her dreams had been shattered and her hopes fulfilled, which left her at war with herself. She had always wanted Angeline to marry someone very important and events had made this impossible, at least in her mind. Then after Angeline came home, Mrs. Dollar hoped that someone would marry her; it didn't really matter who.

I thought it was wonderful because Alfy loved her and I could tell just by looking at her that she loved Alfy; it's the way a marriage should start anyway.

Being sheriff had changed Alfy Hulse somewhat; he was more serious-mannered now, taking his responsibilities with great solemnity. It was just about everyone's opinion that Alfy would be a shoo-in at the next election.

The wedding was a grand affair, even though it hurt Rolle Dollar to pay for it. I made the reception, got my cup of punch, kissed the bride, and found my wife, who had gone to the church for the ceremony.

We took our drinks and found a corner of the lobby away from the crowd. Alfy Hulse found us a few minutes later and came over, looking a bit stiff in a celluloid collar and ascot tie.

"Really a grand affair," I said. "My congratulations." I shifted my cup of punch to the other hand and shook his. "You're looking pretty solemn, Alfy. It wasn't that bad, was it?"

"Wish I could talk to you a minute, Doc. In private."

I glanced at Christina. "Let's go in the kitchen. Will you excuse us, dear?"

We skirted the crowd and stepped into the

150

kitchen; Alfy closed the door. A Mexican dishwasher labored away, humming softly to himself. Alfy said, "Doc, Angeline told me why you took her to Cincinnati, and it's all right with me. I've raised my hell and I'm none too proud of it. Some of Dirty Esther's girls got plenty of my money." He wiped a hand across his mouth. "But this doesn't matter at all, Doc."

"Then what is the problem?"

"Lunsford Cardine came back to town last night."

"The hell you say!"

Alfy nodded. "Butram came to see me late last night at the jail. Lunsford was drunk and passed out, but the old man thinks he's huntin' trouble. Seems he's turned kind of wild. Wears a gun and a big mouth now. The old man claims Lunsford read the engagement announcement in the paper last month. He didn't come back for any good, Doc."

"No, I guess he didn't," I said thoughtfully. "But what can I do about it?"

"I don't want trouble," Alfy said. "But I'm not going to have my wife's name on every dirty mouth in town. Doc, I'll kill him first."

He meant it and I didn't blame him.

So I stood there a moment, trying to figure out something that would save everyone a lot of trouble, then I said, "Alfy, you ought to take Angeline away now. I know it isn't what you planned, but if you both got out of town, it might give some of us a chance to cool Lunsford down and send him on his way."

"Kind of sounds like running."

"Alfy, think of your wife, not your pride."

He nodded. "You're right, Doc. I'll do just that."

I started to open the door for him and heard the buzz of sound from the lobby change tempo; it was a subtle thing, a loss of gaiety. Then Angeline screamed, not loud; it was more an angry bleat than anything and I flung the door open as Alfy elbowed past me.

An avenue had opened up and Angeline was standing in the center of the lobby, trying to break free of Lunsford Cardine's arms.

"That'll do," Alfy said and Lunsford let her go; Angeline rushed sobbing into her father's arms.

Lunsford Cardine was not the same man who had left Victoria. Always as dandified as his father's money could make him, he had found being on his own less than grand. Now he wore range clothes, jeans and a tan brush jacket and a bone-handled pistol on his left hip in a cross-draw holster. A five-day beard stubble hid his cheeks and he looked at Alfy Hulse and laughed.

"You aren't the only man who's put his arms around her," Lunsford said, smiling.

"I said that'll do!"

"Sure. You've gone up in the world and I've

gone down." He looked around the room. "Pretty nice wedding, huh? Pretty little bride, huh? She'll make a nice widow."

Then his hand dropped and scooped up his gun and he shot as the muzzle came hip high; the bullet struck Alfy Hulse in the chest and he staggered back but did not fall. His pistol was under his coat and I think he was reaching for it when Lunsford's bullet caught him, but that didn't stop him.

He fired as he fell and Lunsford grabbed his throat, screamed and whirled and took six stumbling steps outside before falling on the hotel porch.

A few men rushed to him but nearly everyone seemed to converge on Alfy. I was there first, kneeling, opening his vest and shirt and yelling for someone to get something to carry him on. It was a bad wound, very bad, missing the heart but so close that I was certain there was serious damage.

Angeline was nearly hysterical and Christina and some other woman took her away. Someone took down a door and they carefully placed Alfy on it and he was borne out.

Lunsford Cardine was still sprawled on the porch and I could see that he was dead and no one seemed to care about it at all. I ran on ahead to get ready and then a buggy came up behind me and stopped so I could get in; it was Rolle Dollar and

Christina and we went on, Rolle lashing the team.

Alfy was brought into the operating room and I quickly shooed the others out. Christina was cutting away his clothes; he was unconscious, his breathing ragged and bloody and his pulse was weak and erratic.

Christina looked at me and said, "Help him." She had tears in her eyes.

"I can't," I said helplessly. "No one has successfully opened the chest." I wiped my face with a trembling hand. "The bullet's too close to the heart to try to probe."

"Try!" She shouted this.

"He may die if I make one mistake!"

"He's dying now, damn it!" She wasn't angry at me; she was angry at her helplessness and the senseless brutality that had put him there.

We worked frantically, desperately; she operated the sprayer and I scrubbed, then began to probe, carefully, almost with held breath. Christina wiped sweat off my face as I worked, then I felt the bullet, and I prayed fervently that for once I would be given a genuine healer's touch, for once be raised above the level of ignorant, bumbling country doctor appalled at his true lack of knowledge. I prayed for God to reach down and touch both myself and this dying man, to guide my hand and my instrument to a place where mortal eyes couldn't see and to bring out that which was causing him death.

Then I pulled out my probe and dropped the .44 into the pan Christina held waiting.

To describe the remainder of that day and that night is like trying to totally recall a childhood nightmare; I know that we kept carbolic-soaked compresses on the wound and that he somehow hung on, breathing, fighting for his life.

I didn't leave his side, but Christina went out and told the people gathered in front that he was still alive. When night came they were still there and they built a large fire in the street and kept it going through the night. Some people from the Baptist church came and the minister prayed, kneeling in the dust, and they sang hymns— *Jesus, my Lord, my God, my all—we pray to thee.*

Some of the ladies—I never knew who they were—brought coffee and sandwiches for those outside and Christina brought a cup inside to me.

"Tell them he still lives," I said and she went out again.

At dawn they were still there, coming and going, but always returning and I watched Alfy Hulse, watched his fever mount as he fought on, making no sound, no sign, no movement.

I was dreadfully tired, and slept in small increments, sometimes ten minutes, sometimes more, but rarely more than a half hour at a time. Through the day I kept him covered with blankets and kept changing his sterile dressing and in the afternoon I fired up the stove although it was summer and a bake-oven heat was heavy everywhere.

The crowd thinned somewhat during the day and once Christina came in and I think she said that Lunsford Cardine had been quietly buried; I didn't care about him.

Angeline had been outside all that night and finally her father carried her home; it was the only way he could get her to leave and she was too tired to resist.

That night, or perhaps it was early morning—I was too exhausted to look at my watch—Alfy Hulse's fever broke and he stirred and I gave him water immediately. From that moment on he began a slow, steady climb out of the pit, an inch at a time, and when the dawn came I stepped outside, wobbly, almost unable to stand. Fifteen or twenty people stood around, waiting for me to speak.

"He's pretty well out of danger," I said and my voice sounded strange to me. "Go home now. Someone stop at Rolle Dollar's house and tell Alfy's wife."

Then I went back inside and closed the door.

Christina came a short time later; she had a large tin lunch pail and spread the first good meal I'd had in days on a small portable table. Alfy Hulse was breathing regularly and he was resting well. Tomorrow or the next day he would open his eyes and look around and know where he was, and from then on it would only be a matter of time.

"I think," I said, "that if I had put a knife to him he would have died, Christina. It just may be that no one will ever be able to open the chest and have the patient survive."

"You really can't believe that, Ted."

She was right; I didn't, but it all seemed so remote. "I believe that if we'd used an anesthetic he would have died. I'm certain of that. He didn't have the strength to fight off the effect, and any vomiting would have set off the bleeding." I scraped a hand across my bearded face. "When I probed for the bullet I prayed because I was reaching in and touching a man's life. A mistake—"

She smiled and took my hand. "You didn't make any mistakes, Dr. Bodry."

"I take no credit for it."

She got up and went into the room next to my office and turned down the covers of the bed there. Then she came back and helped me off with my vest and shirt and made me stretch out. She took off my shoes and trousers and I kept foolishly insisting that I could do these things for myself and she kept scolding me in that sweet, gentle way she had and that's all I remember because I fell asleep.

When I woke, it was daylight and I sat up and rubbed my eyes. There was a wash stand in the room and I splashed water over my face, toweled dry, then stepped out into the hallway. Christina was in the operating room; Alfy Hulse had not yet been moved to a bed, and when I looked in she was giving him water through a bent glass tube.

"What time is it?" I asked.

"A quarter to eleven," she said and smiled.

"It certainly is remarkable how a few hours sleep will refresh a man."

"Yes," she said. "Especially since you went to bed at a quarter after eight yesterday." Then she came over and put her arms around my neck and gave me one of those soul kisses that could cause so much trouble.

Not with us though.

—14

A physician on the frontier did not have to doctor everyone; a fair percentage of the people doctored themselves, or purchased all medical supplies from the snake oil salesmen who roamed about in their wagons, and although I thought they were an abomination and a pox on the healing arts, I rather enjoyed their shows.

Usually the show was given on the main street, or in the town square and there would be a colored man dressed as some savage from a dark and mysterious continent no one had ever heard of, and usually another man, or a young woman, dressed in veils and possessing all the mystic healing powers of the East.

The "doctor" sold his medicine in bottles, usually a simple concoction largely made up of alcohol, spices, root herbs, and belladonna as a pain killer. Specifically it attacked no general complaint, but it sold for a dollar and up a bottle, depending upon the show, the skill of the barker, and how big a sucker the customer was.

Victoria had her share of medicine men shows; they came to the town long before I did and I suppose the barker felt that I had infringed upon his exclusive territory. But still they came, each year, with their show and bottles and a lot of people, who would never think to come to me with a complaint, bought the medicine.

The doctor got those who had tried these remedies and found them useless. He got trouble very far advanced and because of this his work was difficult, and then I began to see the value of Walter Ivy's "preventive medicine," his continual effort to educate the patient and the family on the necessity of visiting the doctor when they felt only a bit poorly.

This was something I had never done, and didn't particularly believe in, never really understanding that the average man was slightly afraid of a doctor and lacked a doctor's faith in medicine.

159

And this was why I was particularly eager to welcome Dr. O'Brien and Dr. Strudley when they got off the southbound coach. O'Brien was a dumpy man, quite overweight; he had a round florid face eternally cracked into a smile and his hair was brick red. His hand-shake was firm enough to crush the knuckles of a blacksmith and his laugh was a smothered chuckle deep in his chest.

"Doctor Bodry, this is a pleasure," O'Brien said. "Could I get someone to handle the luggage? I have four bags and that large steamer trunk on top."

"The freight agent will bring them to the hospital," I said and turned to Dr. Strudley. He was as English as any man could be. Tall, very military, he wore a bowler and a Grenadier Guard mustache and he carried a silver-headed cane. His grip was firm, polite, reserved; I immediately judged him to be highly competent as well as efficient.

"An honor, sir," Strudley said. He used his cane to point to the other baggage on top of the coach. "Mine, I'm afraid."

With the promise that their luggage would be brought on, I invited them to crowd into my buggy and we drove west to the hospital. They had a good view of it at the end of the street; it was an imposing building and I was immensely proud of it. I parked in front and tied the horse and we went inside, stopping in the foyer. Sunlight reflected brightly from the polished marble and Dr. Strudley said, "Oh, I say!"

"May I show you to your offices and around the building?"

I led them down the hall and paused before a door. The sign said: ARCHIBALD STRUDLEY, M.D.

He looked at it a moment, then opened the door and stepped inside. A good rug muffled his step and he looked at the desk and bookcases and cabinets, all solid walnut, and he gently punched the leather chairs. "This is really quite grand," he said, smiling. "Quite unexpected, sir."

I moved past him and opened another door, then stepped to the other wall and opened one more. "You have two examination rooms, Doctor, each separated by a storage and supply room that is accessible from either room. This assures privacy."

Then I took Dr. O'Brien by the arm. "Your room is just across the hall. If you'll step this way—"

I let them look around and waited in the hallway until they both came out. Down the hall were two more offices and when they saw the names on the doors, I explained that they hadn't arrived yet but I expected both of them in three weeks.

Then I took them on a tour of the first floor—the

second was still completely vacant—and we spent some time in the operating room; they wanted to look at the equipment. Personally I believed it to be the most complete this side of San Francisco, and there were two recovery rooms, and quarters for the surgical nurse or doctor to call.

As we walked deeper into the building, I explained: "At the present time we are using the rest of this floor for hospital facilities. The facilities, when conditions warrant, will be moved to the second floor. Then there is a full basement, which is actually segmented into comfortable quarters. The doctors have a front entrance and the nurses have two side entrances."

Christina stepped out of a door farther down the hall and stopped. "Gentlemen, may I present my wife, Christina. She is my sole nurse until the others arrive later this month." I presented them. "Dr. Strudley. Dr. O'Brien."

Dr. Strudley bowed over her hand and O'Brien held it a bit longer than I thought proper, but I couldn't blame him for that. Christina was a lovely woman, more so now than when we had been married. I knew she was happy. Not as happy as I, to be sure, for I really felt that I was a changed man. I had gained some weight and my disposition had improved one hundred per cent.

"Would you like to visit our patients, gentlemen?" She turned and held open the door and we stepped into Alfy Hulse's room. He was propped up in bed with a third grade reader; he had not been wasting his time and Christina, who taught him when she could, claimed that he was a good pupil.

I took his pulse; it was strong and steady. "How are you feeling, Alfy?"

"Fine, Doc." He looked at Strudley and O'Brien but said nothing.

"Gentlemen, may I introduce our sheriff, Alfred Hulse. Dr. Strudley and Dr. O'Brien." They shook hands and I turned to Christina who had come in with us. "Dear, would you undo the bandage, please."

When she had exposed Alfy's healing wound, both Strudley and O'Brien examined him. "Ugly devil," Strudley said and looked questioningly at me.

"Made by a .44 pistol ball. It had come to rest touching the superior vena cava."

Dr. Strudley's imperturbability broke. "And you probed for that!" He looked at Dr. O'Brien. "Amazing, wouldn't you say, Doctor?"

"Indeed," O'Brien said, thoughtfully. "Tell me, Doctor, do you generally take such risks?"

Before I could answer the door opened and Angeline stepped in. "Oh!" she said, surprised to find us there. I quickly took her arm and hauled her into the room before she could leave. I introduced her and Christina replaced the bandage around Alfy's chest.

"Mrs. Hulse has been a constant companion and a great help these last few weeks," I said. Then I steered them out of the room, and turned them down the hallway.

There were five other patients: a gall stone, a laying-in after a difficult childbirth, a Caesarian section, and two cowboys who had had a fling in Georgia and come back with swamp fever. Fortunately they had been from Spindle and the minute Tennessee Frank found out they were sick he hauled them into town for me and I kept them from spreading it and causing a panic since the symptoms of swamp fever and Yellow Jack are the same.

The only difference being that with one you died and the other you recovered.

It took a few days before Dr. Strudley and Dr. O'Brien got settled in and I took them about town, introducing them to the mayor and the leading citizens and I hired Guy Hulse to drive them on their rounds; I didn't want them getting lost because there was a lot of Texas out there and all the Indians hadn't been run out by Colonel MacKenzie's soldiers.

Still I felt this was the best way to get to know the people, to get out for ten days and make the rounds of the farmers and ranches and see some of the country and sample home cooking and frontier hospitality. They'd learn about Texas politics and Texas troubles and they'd try to decide who was right, the cattlemen or the farmers and they wouldn't be able to make up their minds either.

The end of line of the Texas-Pacific was only twenty-six miles north of town now. We were beginning to feel the impact because some of the engineers stayed at the hotel and the survey crew used Victoria as a base because they were building a roundhouse to the east of town and business was booming like it had never boomed before.

And the last man I expected to see was Walter Ivy.

I was in my office, making up an order for medical supplies when someone knocked, opened the door, and there he was, a little heavier, his hair a little thinner, and certainly more solemn than I had ever seen him.

"Close your mouth, Ted," he said, smiling, flinging his hat in a chair. "This isn't a throat examination."

"What the hell are you doing back?" I asked, crudely, but to the point.

"Ted, do you have room for an older, wiser pill-pusher?" He sat down and crossed his legs, and looked at me as though he were cadging a drink.

"Did Dorsey come back with you?"

He shook his head. "No, I—ah—well, she's pregnant again, Ted. I couldn't persuade her."

I studied him for a moment. "Walter, you never asked her. Isn't that it?"

He tipped his head forward and nodded. "I just couldn't take it anymore, Ted. God, it seemed as though I lost touch with everyone except her parents; she was always over there. Or they were always over to our house." He wiped a hand across his mouth. "Ted, all my life I've had the feeling that I'd be easily smothered. Have you a place for me here?"

"Walter, it wouldn't be the old arrangement; things are too far along for that. I could rent office space to you and you could go back into practice, the same as O'Brien and Strudley are doing." I put my elbows on the desk and clasped my hands. "Walter, what's going to happen when Dorsey comes to her time? Will she come back here or will you pull up stakes and go east again?"

"I don't know," he said. "I hope I have the strength to make her come to me."

"Like the last time?"

"I wish you wouldn't throw that up to me, Ted. I let you down badly, I know."

"I managed."

"Yes, so it seems. Has your practice picked up?"

"Three times what it was seven months ago when you left."

"I suppose I'm still remembered?"

"You know the answer to that."

He got up. "Could you find someplace for me? A back room? A spare closet?"

"Now don't start that throw-me-a-bone-I'm-starving-to-death business, Walter. Your suit cost eighty dollars, at least, and from a private tailor. That watch charm is ruby, isn't it? About a hundred and ninety dollars?" I leaned back in my chair and regarded him carefully. "Walter, you've always managed to take care of yourself very nicely. Your office rent is one hundred dollars a month, just the same as the others. You pay for your own nurse."

"I don't want a nurse, Ted."

"Who's going to take care of your patients?"

"I always have," he said. "That hasn't changed."

"All right." I opened a drawer and gave him a folder. "This is a rate charge for hospitalization, surgery, etc. I think if you'll study that you'll find everything quite equitable."

"My, we certainly are all business, aren't we?" He winked and folded the papers and put them in an inner pocket. "Are you still living in my house?"

"Yes. We've closed off one wing, the old office wing."

"I'd like to move back into it," he said matter of factly. "As soon as possible. I'll set up my office there."

That was a surprise and it stung me; he was

rejecting the hospital and I wasn't sure why. But my pride wouldn't let me argue with him. "All right, Walter. If it wouldn't inconvenience you, could you live in the wing as I used to and give Christina and me a chance to find another house and move out?"

He waved his hand; Walter could be really magnanimous at times.

When I told Christina that Walter was back and that he wanted to move into his house she just snorted through her nose and withheld her opinion, which wasn't very good at best and was getting steadily worse. And I wasn't sure what she disliked, the idea of Walter coming back or leaving a pregnant wife.

It is truly difficult to divine the mind of woman and wise men do not try.

In ten days, Christina and I found a small house on Pearl Street and it had a nice garden and back yard and a carriage shed, and since we were both partial to low, ranch-style adobe, I bought it for sixteen hundred dollars; we moved in immediately and since Mrs. Hempstead had always favored Dorsey and subtly reminded us that we would never have her kind of class, we let her go and she stayed on with Walter Ivy as his housekeeper.

Alfy Hulse was released from the hospital, as were my other patients, but somehow the beds never remained vacant long. Dr. Strudley and Dr.

O'Brien were partially responsible for this because they had both practiced in large hospitals and understood the advantages of hospital care and urged their patients to forsake home treatment. Thank God the nurses arrived. Five of them and they came south on the train; end of track was now the roundhouse while a new depot and freight shed was being built. The one who immediately impressed me was Mrs. Murdock, a woman in her late forties, English, unbelievably proper, and as grim a person as I've ever seen. She inspected the hospital like a field commander looking over the sorriest troops ever to be inflicted upon his command. Nothing was right. The place was not nearly clean enough to suit her and there wasn't a decently made up bed in the place, or certainly not neat enough to suit her.

Hercules in the Augean stables was a doddering old swamper compared to a determined woman attacking dirt. Mrs. Murdock could bark orders like a top sergeant and there was no doubt in my mind, or in the minds of the other nurses, who was going to be head "cap" around there.

Mrs. Murdock, an amazing woman; she would even have been an amazing man. Married to a lieutenant in the Coldstream Guards who had fallen in 1856 in the Crimean War, she was left with two small children and only a small pittance from the Crown. She dedicated herself to helping the sick and bedridden, learned by practice, and soon advanced to formal nursing.

With her children grown and happily married, she came to America, and then she came to me, I'm happy to say.

In one week's time she knew every nook and cranny of the hospital, could recite from memory the inventory of my supply rooms, and at all times knew every detail of everything that went on.

The great stone face could instantly cow the roughest cowboy. Yet I noticed that no child ever showed the slightest fear of her, for she had the gentlest hands and it was not uncommon for a crying infant to stop when she brushed its forehead.

——15

The railroad certainly brought prosperity to Victoria and the war-tattered economy of Texas was finally on a firm and independent footing. Cattlemen now drove to the loading pens and sold to the local buyers; the day of the big drives was nearing an end although in isolated parts of the state, they still went north with the herds each spring.

Most all the ranchers and farmers had put down wells and now the windmill salesmen came and before fall, you could see them, whirling land-marks where once there had been nothing but rolling land and grass.

If a man had the time it was pleasurable to go down to the depot and watch a freight train being unloaded. Shining John Deere plows and harrows and new buggies and wagons. Prices on many items in Rolle Dollar's store came down, especially the breakable items; the railroad was just not as rough as freight lines and items could be less expensively packed.

Then a flatcar came in and was put on the siding and it changed everyone's life in some way. In many cases it ended life.

The flatcar contained barbed-wire, the first any of us had ever seen.

At first everyone thought it was for Rolle Dollar, and an angry group of cattlemen converged on his store to have words with him. But the wire didn't belong to him; he had earlier thrown the sales-man out of the place and refused to handle it.

So an independent store had opened up in a back room.

The salesman was a representative of a wire company from Peoria, Illinois, and he had four helpers, four of the toughest looking men I had ever seen. They all stood six foot four in their stocking feet and they wore derbies and high, turtle-necked sweaters and carried brass knuckles and the cowboys hated them.

But none of the cowboys wanted to fight with them.

These gentlemen made certain that the wire was safely transported from the railroad siding to the warehouse in back of Bingham's saddle shop—and Bingham, who had only rented the barn because the money was good, was all but an outcast.

Farmers made their purchases there and the helpers loaded the wagons and escorted the farmers out of town, riding a sort of shotgun to the farm, and there unloading the wire.

The salesman made a lot of money because there was no doubt in anyone's mind that the barbed wire was superior to the old single-strand stuff. And any steer driven into the wire would be torn pretty badly.

So the veterinarian was bound to pick up a little business there.

George Thursday, a young El Paso lawyer who had moved to town six months before, handled all the books for the hospital—his practice was not yet so extensive that an outside job insulted him.

I mention this because people were paying their bills. Not only the current ones, but for services rendered up to two years before. These Texans had their pride and they knew that ten dollars wasn't the usual fee for delivering a baby, so they came in and paid me the other forty and went back home feeling square with the world.

And the Mercy Hospital's account at Cardine's bank crept into the black.

Well into the black.

But it seemed that the hospital routine would just never settle down, and then it dawned on me that it never would. Dr. Fred Ellsworth, a young surgeon from Chicago arrived. So did Dr. Linus McCaffe, a physician from Baltimore; he was a friend of Walter's, a robust out-going man not above talking about someone else's business.

It was obvious to me that we were going to have to furnish the second floor before winter, and that wasn't far off. Until now we had ordered all meals for the patients and staff from the hotel; they were brought to and fro in a dogcart, and Mrs. Murdock didn't like that at all.

Walter Ivy, I'm sure, would have immediately labeled her a meddler, a complainer, but I found that everything she said made sense, and Mrs. Murdock wanted a kitchen and dining room for the staff installed in the basement.

A little figuring soon pointed out that her argument would save us a good deal of money in the long run. So we consulted Rolle Dollar and sent to Kansas City for the equipment and Mrs. Murdock handled the hiring of personnel; she must have interviewed forty people carefully before selecting six, all negro.

This caused me a moment of concern, for although I had not picked up any southern prejudices, I knew how strongly the feelings of these people ran and little bothered them more than negroes running around and not belonging to anyone. Mrs. Murdock was firm as only she could be, and I let the matter go.

I was asked to attend a meeting of the county supervisors, not an unusual thing, so I had an early dinner with my wife and walked over to the courthouse. Walter Ivy was there, which didn't surprise me much; he had been getting back into the old swing again and I only saw him now and then since his practice kept him pretty busy.

When I came in he looked around and patted a chair near him so I went over and sat down. The small room was choking with cigar smoke and the supervisors were arguing over the cost of cement sidewalks along main street. I listened to the pros and cons of it and finally they had a vote; the sidewalks would go in as soon as bids could be let.

There was a man there I didn't know, and finally he was identified as Prentiss Chalmbers, of the Edison Electric Company. Mr. Chalmbers was an engineer and he wanted to sell the county board on having an electric light plant built and street lights installed. For better than forty minutes he displayed graphs and charts and explained that a power company could, in twenty years, amortize the investment through sale of electrical power to individual customers.

Walter thought all this was boring as hell, but I was interested.

But Mr. Chalmbers didn't make his sale; unanimously the board felt that people were perfectly satisfied with coal oil lamps and that seemed to be that.

He gathered his charts and briefcases and as he passed down the aisle, I touched his sleeve and he stopped. "I'm Dr. Bodry. Would you meet me in the hotel bar, say in an hour, for a drink?"

"Delighted, Doctor." He nodded and went out.

Came then the matter for which the supervisors felt that my presence was needed.

My bill for the care of Sheriff Alfred Hulse.

Mike Sharniki, who was the chairman said, "Doc, this here bill is a little steep, ain't it? Four hundred and seventy dollars?"

"I thought it was very clearly itemized," I said. "Alfy was in the hospital for thirty-two days, and for the first week he required almost constant day and night care. At ten dollars a day I think that's most reasonable. Your wife thought so when she had that miscarriage two months ago."

He wasn't going to argue about that I could see. "Well all right, doc. It says here your fee is a hundred and fifty dollars. As I recall it took you all of fifteen minutes to get the bullet out of him."

Walter J. Ivy cleared his throat and everyone looked at him. He said, "It seems to me that Dr.

Bodry's error is not breaking the bill down to component parts. Now I would have charged a dollar for taking the bullet out."

There was an instant buzz of talk, which stopped instantly when he said, "However," and he waited for silence to run on a bit. "However, I would have charged you three hundred dollars for knowing where to dig for it. That's really not much for a good man's life, and I trust no one here is going to say that Alfy Hulse is not a good man. Best lawman we ever had!"

Someone moved that they pay the bill, and it was seconded and passed. Walter and I left right after that and as we walked across the lawn, he said, "You need someone to collect for you."

"Walter, I never once doubted your power of persuasion."

We reached the corner where he turned and he stopped to light a cigar. "Ted, thanks for turning some of the collections over to me. I'd have never known if—"

"I would have, Walter. Are you spending a good deal of time in the country?"

"You know me, the wandering pill peddler."

"What do you hear from Dorsey?"

It was a question he hadn't wanted me to ask, but I didn't care about that. He pursed his lips and shot up his eyebrows. "Not much. To be honest she hasn't answered my letters. Damn it, what kind of a wife is she anyway?"

"She's probably asking the same kind of question about you."

He laughed although it wasn't funny to him. "I heard that Dr. McCaffe arrived. He's a good man, if you can stand him. I think he came from a large Irish family of seventeen where no one had any privacy or secrets; he just can't mind his own business."

"Is he a trouble maker?"

"Oh, no, no, no, no, nothing like that."

He started to turn away and I took his sleeve. "Walter, why don't you ask him how Dorsey's getting along?"

"Perhaps," Walter said, "if I happen to run into him." Then he turned and walked slowly down the dark street and I thought: now there goes an unhappy man, and a damned fool.

At the hotel bar I found Prentiss Chalmbers and we took our drinks to a table. "I was very interested in what you had to say tonight."

He laughed. "It's too bad I can't say the same for the board. Ah, well, time is on my side. We're in the process of putting in electricity in San Antonio and Dallas. Other towns will follow. It's inevitable."

"I had some experience with electric lights in Baltimore," I said. "They impressed me as being highly superior to lamps, even with surgical reflectors." I leaned forward. "Mr. Chalmbers, I run a hospital and if you can spare the time before you leave, I would like you to look over the building and discuss the possibilities. We have a steam boiler in the basement now for heat and hot water. Perhaps—"

He smiled. "A small dynamo and steam engine just to furnish light for the hospital?"

"Yes."

He thought about it a moment. "Could I look at it now? I really would like to take the morning train because I have an afternoon appointment in Austin."

I paid for the drinks and we left the hotel together.

At the hospital I introduced him to Mrs. Murdock; I hadn't thought for a moment that I could have escorted him through without her knowing about it. And she got a lamp and went on ahead of us into the basement.

Chalmbers inspected the furnace and the flue and made many calculations on a note pad; we spent thirty minutes while he poked around and asked questions about the walls and floors. Finally we went back to my office and Mrs. Murdock left us.

I gave Chalmbers a cigar and a light; he settled back in a chair and said, "I would say a little over four thousand dollars. Of course that includes shipping, installation, and an electric motor to convert your pull elevator to electric. Electricity is power, Doctor, not just light. It does useful work."

I shook my head. "I just couldn't go that much money, Mr. Chalmbers. Perhaps in another year—"

"Your bank—"

"No, I'm in debt for twenty thousand dollars now. Private loan."

He laid one of his business cards on my desk. "Doctor, I must catch the train, but talk to your backers. Four thousand dollars is not a lot of money considering the investment you already have. Please exhaust a few possibilities before giving up the idea." He got up and buttoned his coat. "Wire me at the Senator in Austin. I'll be there three days." He drew deeply on his cigar. "Doctor, let me make you a proposition. It's been my observation that doctors are pretty influential people in a community. A doctor gets a new buggy and it isn't long before someone else buys one. I want to sell Victoria on electric lights. All right, I'll go through the back door if I must. I'll refigure this so that installation and equipment is at our cost, and run electric lights to your home from here." He winked, and smiled. "In a year, or less, my company will be back to install them for the town. I'd take that gamble."

"In round numbers, what would that figure be?"

"About three thousand dollars."

It set me to pacing around the office; the gamble was there, and it looked good to me, a risk that I believed would pay off. It meant that I

179

wouldn't be able to buy one piece of equipment for eight months, and I'd have to talk Butram Cardine into a personal loan, but I believed I could swing that. So I turned to Prentiss Chalmbers and said, "I'll wire you the money in Austin. Is that satisfactory?"

"Perfectly. And I'll come back, make up specifications, and sign the contracts. I want you to understand that this unit, boiler, engine, and dynamo, is not simply a basic unit. It should be ample to handle your needs and expanded applications for many years. It's not wise to try to get by. Never open up a possibility of overloading the equipment."

I saw him to the door and shook hands with him, and after he left I checked with Mrs. Murdock and went home.

Christina was in the parlor, wrapped in a wooly robe, curled in the big chair with a book. She put it down when I kissed her then she got up and went to the kitchen, bringing back a tray with coffee and peach pie.

"What's new and exciting with the county board?"

"They paid Alfy's bill," I said.

"Good."

"They also turned down a proposition from the Edison Electric company to put up electric lights."

She thought about it a moment. "It would be

nice, wouldn't it? But I suppose it's expensive. Everything nice is."

"I talked to the representative," I said. "As a matter of fact, if I can get a loan from Cardine, I'm going to have a plant put in the basement of the hospital." Then I told her how much and took some of the joy out of it.

"Do you think you ought to—well, go deeper in debt?"

"That really doesn't worry me," I said. "Christina, all I've seen this country do is grow. Really. The railroad's come here and people have come here. Why, two years ago when I rode south and found that family killed by Indians, all the country there was prairie. Now there's eight farms out there, with houses and barns and fences up and crops growing. Look at the town. Why this spring alone there were eleven new houses built. Everything's growing, Christina. I've just got to grow with it."

"Ted, I wouldn't hold you back. You know that." She put her arms around me and kissed me, then raised an eyebrow. "Everything's growing, but we're not raising a family. Got something against kids?"

"I'm trying. I'm trying," I said, holding back a smile.

"Try harder."

"Oftener?"

She smiled. "That too."

——16

If I had known anything at all about railroads I would have realized that the roundhouse switch yards meant something, but my knowledge is limited to riding on the trains. So when Murray McCloud, the division superintendent, called on me, it was somewhat of a surprise and I wasn't sure exactly what he wanted.

McCloud was an eastern man and spoke with a real Yankee twang, but he was blunt and to the point, and he liked business first and his fun second. He wore corduroy pants and jacket and flat-heeled boots and he had dirt under his fingernails, which immediately impressed me for I am partial to supers who work.

He had a map and unrolled it on my desk, then placed his finger on Victoria. "This is going to be our terminal. As you know, end of track is now pushing southeast to Port Lavaca. The survey crew is working now in the vicinity of Goliad, to the southwest. By summer of next year we'll have a rail down to Gussettville and Laredo on the border. And from the Gussettville junction we'll have lines to Rio Grande City and Brownsville." He folded the map and put it on the floor. "That means we're talking about a crew of three thousand men, Doctor. Quite naturally we have our own physicians and emergency facilities; they're always getting hurt. Railroad building is not a safe occupation. However, our facilities are limited. Always have been and always will be. We just cannot hospitalize the injured. No place to put them. Therefore, the railroad would like to enter into negotiation with you for the care of these men."

The possibilities of this rather staggered me, but I tried to act as though I discussed these things every day. "Mr. McCloud, what are the percentages? Your accident rate in ratio to the number of workers employed?"

"Around six and a quarter per cent," he said, drawing a notebook from an inner pocket. He consulted it. "Eighty per cent of those are fractures, abrasions, and crushing accidents. Eleven per cent are injuries due to strain. The rest, general failure of health through disease." His manner brightened. "We are not particularly bothered by social diseases, Doctor, because we take care to clean up the towns we work near. A dirty red-light district can put half the crew down with runny peters, to put it bluntly."

I jotted these figures down on a pad. "Exactly how would you like for me to proceed, Mr. McCloud?"

"The railroad is not interested in bogging down further with more paperwork, Doctor. That is to say, we're not in favor of a rate that is based on individual injuries or diseases. What we want is an overall, blanket charge that will cover everything." He leaned his forearms on my desk. "Understand, Doctor, that every patient you get from us will require hospitalization. We understand this, so we expect to pay for it. But any railroad that wants to stay in business knows that to get good workers and keep them you have to feed well and take care of them."

"I'll discuss this with my colleagues immediately," I promised. "Where can I get in touch with you?"

"I'm just moving into my office near the roundhouse," McCloud said. He offered his hand. "Call on me there. And if I'm out, the chief clerk will know where to find me or get in touch with me."

I walked with him to the door, then went back to my office and worked for several hours, jotting down figures. Of necessity I had to work from the percentages of fracture cases, which predominated as to injury type. And then I had to compute on the most serious, leg and rib fractures, to arrive at a stable fee.

Finally I sent for Mrs. Murdock and she made certain the other doctors were notified of a four o'clock meeting; I requested that they all rearrange their schedules and be there.

I even invited Walter J. Ivy, although I didn't expect him to respond.

And I should have known better than to figure that because he came to my office ten minutes later. Fred Ellsworth arrived and Mrs. Murdock brought him an extra chair. Then McCaffe, O'Brien, and Strudley came in and sat down and I explained in detail the proposition offered by the railroad.

No one doubted that it was a good thing; it could be a bonanza that would, for over a year, guarantee the hospital a substantial income. I gave them the figures I had come up with and then we broke them down carefully, taking first the fee for hospitalization.

Dr. Archibald Strudley had an opinion: "Our standard fee is ten dollars a day, and four more for a special night nurse if around the clock attendance is required. You've quoted ten dollars straight across the board, Ted, and I jolly well think that's a bit high. Eight would be more in line, you know. I was resident in Charing Cross and on the main the average nurse can quite capably handle eight average bed patients. And the more you have, old boy, the less expensive it is. Ten dollars a day wouldn't near cover the cost of home care, while in the hospital it's ample."

"I'm inclined to agree," O'Brien said. "Archie's figure of eight dollars seems most reasonable. Good for us and good for the railroad."

Walter Ivy cleared his throat but no one paid any attention to him.

"You have the averages working for you, old boy," Strudley said. "According to the figures you've outlined, we should have eighteen or twenty beds constantly occupied. That's two thirds of the second floor. That would average out to two hundred dollars a day."

"All right, eight dollars then."

We discussed in length the other facets, surgeon's fees, physician's fees, cost of the operating room, and once in a while Walter Ivy would clear his throat and finally Archibald turned and glared at him, his handlebar mustache bristling.

"Well, sir?" he demanded, with unnecessary emphasis.

Walter Ivy's head came up and he looked at Strudley for nearly a minute and I had never seen him with that expression; he was like a little boy who had been unruly in class.

He got up and said, "If you'll excuse me, I have calls to make."

"Walter," I said quickly, "I wish you wouldn't go."

"I can contribute nothing here," he said and walked out.

Strudley swiveled around in his seat to watch him, then said, "What a ruddy bore."

It was on the tip of my tongue to contradict him, but I held back, suddenly realizing that Strudley was more right than wrong. Walter Ivy, in the presence of these men, did not come to the forefront, and this saddened me considerably.

Still there was business to get on with and it was a quarter to six before we hammered it all out, the blanket fee which would cover everything from a mashed toe to the most serious abdominal surgery.

Eighteen dollars and seventy-five cents a day.

George Thursday came to my house after supper that night and we sat in the parlor until quite late, preparing the first draft of the contracts; he intended to have them ready the next day and take them to Murray McCloud himself.

It was very late when he left and Christina had already gone to bed, but I wasn't ready to sleep, so I got my hat and coat and walked across town to Walter Ivy's house.

The lamps were still on in the parlor and I knocked; he came to the door a moment later and seemed surprised to see me. "Come in, Ted. I was reading."

As I stepped into the parlor I could see no book or paper and knew that he hadn't been reading, but it was none of my business. "May I offer you a drink, Ted?"

"Thanks, Walter. Whiskey and water." I sat down and put my hat on a side table. "How is Dorsey?"

"Well. I got a letter from her father. Not very

friendly in tone, but informative. She's going abroad for two months with her parents. England and France." He came back and handed me my drink. "What brings you out tonight, Ted?"

"Just hungry for some talk, I guess. Old ties and all that."

He bunched his eyebrows. "It seems to me the old ties are pretty well broken, Ted."

"Walter, that sounds a little petulant. I do wish you'd forget that incident this afternoon. Strudley is a little crabby and gruff by nature, but he's a good man."

"I consider his an insufferable ass!" Walter said, with surprising vehemence. "It seems to be the pattern with a man who's been to Oxford, Leipzig, or Zurich. They know it all and anyone else's opinion isn't worth a tiddly-damn." He hoisted his drink and tossed it off, straight.

For a few moments the ticking of the hall clock was the only thing that broke the silence, then I said, "Walter, I wish you'd reconsider and join the hospital staff. You'd find the arrangement quite satisfactory."

"Do you really think so? A man must be his own boss, Ted." He shook his head. "I wouldn't be worth anything in staff conference; you saw that this afternoon. I was an outsider and they damned well showed me my place." He splayed his fingers against the leather arms of the chair. "Ted, I believe in home care for my patients. I believe that a member of the family can offer the patient far more through love and devotion than any nurse, no matter how well she's trained. It is a gospel with me, Ted. The natural way for a woman to give birth is in her bed, in her own home, attended by a mid-wife or a friend, not some disinterested, sterile, hatchet-face who happened to go to school to learn how to carry a bedpan. It is just as simple as that."

"Walter, I've never for an instant considered you a foolish man. Please don't make me revise that opinion now."

"Revise what you damned please," he said. "I'm not like you, Ted; I don't automatically believe that every change, every step of progress is for the best. I love medicine, the country doctor, call-me-any-hour-of-the-day-or-night kind of medicine. I'm not dazzled by polished marble floors and a nurse in a starched uniform. Pomp and ceremony is for the military, Ted. You can't run the heart on a schedule."

I sighed and picked up my hat. "I'm sorry I disturbed you, Walter."

He smiled unexpectedly. "Walking out on an argument, Ted?"

"There doesn't seem to be much point in continuing it. But you're turning into a disappointed man, Walter. For God's sake, and your own, I wish you'd reach some reconciliation with your wife."

"That wouldn't be hard. I could go back to her."

"Can't you do that?"

He shook his head.

"Good night, Walter."

I let myself out and walked slowly back to my house. The hall lamp was still burning, although it sputtered, nearly out of kerosene; I blew it out and walked quietly up the stairs, trying not to wake my wife.

She was awake, propped up in bed, reading; she put the magazine down when I came in and I undressed. "Did you go to see Walter?" I must have looked surprised, for she laughed. "After you left the house I wondered where you would go, then I guessed that it would be Walter's. And if you called this late, it meant that you were bothered by something serious. A disagreement?"

"The man needs his wife. If he had any sense he'd go back to her."

"If she had any sense she'd be here," Christina said. "Ted, it's the man that makes the woman happy and content, not the house or the place where the house is built." She grew thoughtful. "I think it's his son. He needs the boy. Walter's a natural-born father, Ted. He'd spoil the boy rotten, but he's that way. He's got to give love and when he's denied that, he turns sour."

"I never thought of it that way."

"Well, isn't it that way? The army for many

years, that was his love. Then you. Why did he single you out, Ted?"

I thought about it, then smiled, "Because of my singular brilliance? No?"

"No."

"That's a crushing thing to say to a husband. Did you know that the top of your nightgown is unlaced?"

"Don't change the subject."

"That material is quite sheer, isn't it?" I sat on the edge of the bed and put my arms around her and she half tried to push me away.

"You are just not concentrating," she said.

"Oh, but I am!" I said and blew out the light.

She giggled when I slid under the covers.

A wire to Prentiss Chalmbers caught him at the hotel in Austin; my proposition was simple and put very straight forward: I wanted the electric dynamo and would buy it if the company would extend a line of credit. I would make my first payment, one third of the amount, ninety days after the plant was installed, and two equal payments one month apart.

Late in the afternoon I got an answer from Chalmbers; the equipment would be shipped from Buffalo, New York within ten days for he had wired in the order and recommended that the credit arrangement be approved. I could expect the workmen in two weeks to install the base for

191

the dynamo and steam engine, and put in the wiring and fixtures.

Perhaps I was taking a chance, counting my chickens before the eggs had been laid, but I felt completely confident that the Texas-Pacific Railroad would sign the contracts I had offered. If they didn't, then I'd try to negotiate a personal loan at the bank. Butram Cardine was not exactly a friend, but he wasn't an enemy either. The death of his son had made him very solemn, and he constantly wore a mantle of shame, as though his son's downfall was really his fault.

When a man feels that way, the best thing to do is to leave him alone.

The Texas Rangers had set up a tent camp about a half-mile north of town, and increased their number to seven, all gaunt, hard-eyed men who walked softly and made people jump when they spoke. The fence cutting went on, but it was not as wide-spread as it had been, mainly due to the rangers constantly patrolling, and Alfy Hulse's deputies on the move all the time.

And Alfy was back on the job, gaining weight now to where you could hardly know that he'd had both feet in death's door. I saw him now and then and twice I went to his house on Sycamore Street to see Angeline. Marriage agreed with her; she was getting plump and was constantly gay and hoping that she'd hurry up and get pregnant because she knew that Alfy would be a wonderful father.

Why do women always think that? In town alone I knew a hundred men who were terrible fathers.

And some women who were worse mothers.

But in the beginning they all thought they were going to be wonderful.

With Angeline and Alfy I had no doubt at all. All the giddy, little girl–teasing ways she had once had and which had irritated me so much were gone. She kept a neat house, cooked well, and knew how to make Alfy come home nights.

And it made me wonder if she hadn't really reduced the good things in life down to the basics and not cluttered them up as Dorsey cluttered her life. And Walter's.

Some people just couldn't remember that it was good to be alive.

—17

Since it is a general feeling in Texas to ignore Mexicans, I do not hold anyone at fault that the Mexican boy who had been shot down on Victoria's main street was quickly put out of mind, and once Scotty Breedon paid his fine and served his time in the jail, he went back to work as though it had never happened.

Only the Mexicans working for Will Stang

didn't forget it and they paid pretty close attention to their fences, taking turns each night to guard them. The fence cutters were still pretty busy and you might wonder why all the fuss about a little cut wire. Perhaps it is best appreciated if one realizes that ten per cent of a farmer's total investment goes into his fences. Digging post holes is a tedious, slow job; they must be set straight and even and the job is usually laid out by a surveyor to make certain you're not on someone else's land. Then the wire has to be strung, stretched and stapled so that it does not sag. All this costs money and a good deal of it.

A cut wire means more than splicing; it means restringing for a hundred yards, and a little of this can soon run a farmer into the hole since he's working hard to get a foothold to begin with.

So with the two Mexicans alternating patrol on Will Stang's fence it was only natural that sooner or later they were going to meet up with the wire cutters.

It was one of those starry, black, moonless fall nights and the wire cutters, Scotty Breedon, his brother, Jonas, and a cousin called Jim-John bellied up to Will Stang's fence with cutters in hand. And the mysterious hand of fate which stirs us all gave a peculiar swirl to it then and brought Jesus Garcia and his double-barreled shotgun to that point as Scotty Breedon snipped the first wire. It sang when it parted and Jim-John swore when a barb cut the back of his hand.

Those two sounds were enough for Jesus Garcia; he was no more than twenty yards distant and he pointed his shotgun down toward the ground and fired: BAM! BAM! as quickly as he could pull the triggers.

The first charge of buckshot caught Scotty Breedon and his brother, Jonas. Scotty took most of the charge in the head and chest and died instantly, and Jonas, badly wounded and partially blinded, got up and ran stumbling across the prairie, searching for where he had left his horse.

Jim-John, badly frightened, jumped up and Garcia's second charge took him through the lower legs and he fell, screaming and rolling.

The unaccustomed violence and Jim-John's screaming frightened Jesus Garcia and he dropped the shotgun and ran toward the house about three-quarters of a mile away. Of course the shooting woke Stang and his wife and Garcia's cousin, but he reached the yard by the time they dressed and rolled out and lit lanterns.

It took a minute or two to calm Garcia and get the straight of it, but then Stang put him on a horse and sent him to town for the sheriff and doctor while he and Garcia's cousin took lanterns and a wagon and went out to find the wounded men.

Alfy Hulse woke me and told me quickly what

had happened; he had a saddle horse waiting for me outside. When I came out, Sergeant Burkhauser and two other Texas Rangers were mounted up and ready to go; we left together and wasted no time getting to the Stang place. Mrs. Stang, a pretty woman in her thirties, was on the porch and she pointed as we rode up, indicating the south pasture and we went there, guided by the lanterns bobbing about.

"Thank God you got here," Stang said as we dismounted. Scotty Breedon lay pretty much as he had fallen, wire cutters still in hand. His brother was gone, but Jim-John lay ten yards away, dead now. His left leg had been nearly blown off at the knee and the right one would have been beyond saving; he had bled to death trying to drag himself back to where they had left the horses.

Sergeant Burkhauser, with a lantern and the instincts of a fine hunting dog, said, "There were three. The other one's wounded. Better come with us, Doc. You goin' to stay here and get the straight of this, sheriff?"

"Yes," Hulse said.

"Where's Jesus Garcia?" Stang asked.

"He wanted to wait in town," Hulse said.

A ranger brought up our horses through the break in the fence and we swung up and started trailing the wounded man, Burkhauser leading the way. We found the place where the horses had been picketed, and blood on the grass; the horses, a bit frightened by the smell of blood, had reared and pulled their pins, but the trail ended so we assumed that the third man had caught up his horse and managed to haul himself aboard.

Burkhauser picked up the tracks of the horse and once a direction was established, Burkhauser blew out the lantern. He lit a cigar and said, "This is Circle B graze. Let's pay a call on Sam Usher."

I wondered why he had waited this long to identify the brand; we all knew who Scotty and Jonas Breedon worked for, but then I realized that Burkhauser had held open the possibility that the third man had worked for another brand.

Now that he was certain, he lifted his horse into a trot and two miles later we came into the dark yard; there was no light showing anywhere.

A voice from the vicinity of the porch said, "There's a dozen rifles trained on you so move easy!"

"This is Burkhauser, Texas Rangers! And you'd damned well better put those rifles up in a hurry and strike a light!"

He had a bull voice and there was a flurry on the porch, then several lanterns were lit and Sam Usher and his son stepped into the yard, holding the lantern up so he could see.

"What the hell you want here?" Usher asked.

He was a typical Texas cattleman, as lean as a razor back hog, tough as a saddle, and he held little fear of man or beast.

"A little fence cuttin'," Finley Burkhauser said, stepping from the saddle. "Scotty and Jonas Breedon are dead, Sam. We think the third man made it back. Brought Doc Bodry along."

"No one here," Usher maintained.

"Don't be a fool now, Sam," Burkhauser advised. "We'll make the fence-cutting charge stick so why let a man die because you can't let go of a thing?"

Usher's son shifted his feet and moved his hand an inch closer to the butt of his pistol; Burkhauser said, "Sonny, it would grieve me to have to shoot a young fella like you, but things are a bit touchy right now and I'd have to figure any move you made was hostile. So if you get to jerkin' your hands I'll have to blow you plumb in half." He looked steadily at the boy, then switched his attention to Sam Usher. "Well, Sam, you don't have all night about this."

"He's in the bunkhouse," Usher said wearily. "The boys are with him but I don't think it's any use."

I didn't give a damn for his opinion; I turned and trotted across the yard and rushed into the bunkhouse, ignoring the pistols suddenly pointed my way. Then I saw the man, a blanket completely covering him.

One of the cowboys said, "You're ten minutes too late, Doc."

"I didn't want to be," I said angrily. "Sam wanted to jaw in the yard."

"Well, he made it back," another said. "That's what he wanted, I guess." He looked at me. "Scotty and Jim-John?"

"Dead," I said and walked out.

Everyone was in Usher's house; his wife was making coffee and Burkhauser was asking questions and writing the answers down in a notebook. Then he snapped it shut and put it in his pocket. "Sam, I want you to come into town in the morning and turn yourself in to Alfy Hulse. We'll get the judge to hold a hearing and set bail. Now you understand I'm bein' reasonable about this. Don't make us come after you."

Sam Usher nodded. "All right, Burkhauser. I'll be there."

"I guess there's no more here," Burkhauser said and the two rangers with him went outside. "Sam, Sam, you damned fool. If you caught a man rustlin' your beef, you'd hang him. Don't you think this is just as serious? Or did you figure that it wasn't because he was a farmer?"

Usher's expression turned bleak. "I don't want to go to prison, Burkhauser!"

"You be in town in the morning or I'll have every law officer in the state of Texas after you," Burkhauser said and turned to the door. He stopped there. "Tell me something, Sam: do you think Scotty got what was coming to him for killing that Mexican?"

"It seemed a little stiff to me," Usher said. "The fine was enough; I had to borrow to pay it."

"Well that boy's cousin killed your men after they cut Stang's fence," Burkhauser said. "Now who the hell do you think the joke's on?"

He brushed past me and went out and I followed him and we mounted for the ride back. We rode along a way, then he said, "Sometimes I just don't understand a man's thinkin' at all, Doc. Usher's a good man, but he just can't get things in the right perspective and believe that a farmer has the same rights he has."

"Sergeant, what do you think a jury will do?"

"It's hard to say, Doc. People have been livin' under this threat of violence for some months now and they're gettin' tired of it. Could be that they'll hit Sam Usher hard and let that be a warnin'. Or they might let him go."

"They do that," I said, "and there'll be more fences cut and more men killed."

The jury deliberated for two hours; they did not let Sam Usher go. He was fined fifteen-hundred dollars and given two years in Huntsville prison, a verdict which outraged many of the cattlemen, yet impressed them that high-handed methods were going out of style in Texas.

It was the beginning of the end of a long reign for the man on horseback; the man on the street had a voice and he was using it and none of the cattlemen were stupid enough to think that they could swing an election and buy the law on their side.

So the wire cutters, like the illegal running iron, went into the bottom of feed bins and haymows and there was no more wire cutting. In November the Texas Rangers departed and the land settled down to the winter, which gave every indication of being mild.

The summer had been reasonably cool, with now and then thunder showers breaking up the hot spells and keeping the creeks up; it was what old timers would someday call a good summer, and I suppose, on the main, it was.

It was a good summer for me, both professionally and personally satisfying, since the hospital was increasingly becoming the Mecca for the sick and we had patients come from as far as Abilene and Jefferson for operations or treatment.

Certainly one of the sensations—and old timers still talk about it—was the evening when Prentiss Chalmbers closed a switch in the basement of the hospital and the dynamo hummed and electric lights came on all over the building and pushed the night completely away. In front, over the main entrance, a cluster of frosted glass globes flooded the brick walk with light and the crowd gathered there gasped, then cheered.

I went home immediately; Christina was waiting for me and the house was dark. Inside the door I turned a porcelain switch and the parlor lights came on, brighter than fifteen lamps, and we went through the house, turning on the lights and marveling at the wonderful brightness of it all.

"I've never seen them before," she said softly, almost crying. "It's like the day never ends, isn't it?"

Aaron Stiles, who liked a bit of controversy anyway, wrote a lengthy article in the Victoria paper and chided the county board for being so short sighted that the town as the whole didn't enjoy this blessing.

It was a good article and Christina clipped it out and put it away.

Electric lights in the hospital opened new horizons for us and took much of the terror out of night emergency cases, if you can imagine what it is like performing a tracheotomy on a four year old choking on a button and nothing to illuminate your work but a kerosene lamp. Ward duty became easier for lamps are cumbersome and you either leave them on and waste kerosene or you're always lighting and blowing them out.

The lights pulsated slightly; you noticed this right away, but in fifteen minutes you forgot about it and could read without strain and operate without fear.

Everyone seemed very enthusiastic about the lights and most of the town council and county supervisors came around for their tour of the plant in the basement and they would stand there and watch the brass governor balls on the steam engine whir around and listen to the hum of the dynamo and shake their heads at the incomprehensible miracle of it all.

Guy Hulse, who worked full time as ambulance driver, janitor, and general handy man, was given an intensive course by Prentiss Chalmbers in the care and maintenance of the plant, and although it was beyond my understanding, Guy could shut the plant down in the daytime, change light-bulbs, rewire switches, rig extra lights for special use, and make repairs on the dynamo when they were needed. He didn't understand anything about electricity except that it was like water through pipes; if you kept the flow uninterrupted every-thing worked fine.

Mechanical aptitude, which Guy had in abundance, was a dark, mysterious tangle for me and I could not replace the nut on a buggy axle without cross threading it.

I rather expected Walter Ivy to say something to me about the lights, but he did not. He came around one evening, looked at the cluster of out-side lights a moment, then walked to Mulligan's saloon and began his evening drinking. Alfy Hulse spoke to me about this because Walter was carrying this on a little too far and too steadily and once Alfy had had to escort him home while Walter sang old cavalry songs in a loud, off-key voice.

We didn't see much of one another; he still practiced in the county, keeping his office in the wing of the old house, and he never brought a patient to me. He lost a few; doctors have to learn to live with that, and I never heard anyone blame him because death is understood by all people.

He came to me one night when I was in my office, studying some journals; I looked up to see who had opened my door without knocking for no one on the hospital staff ever did that.

He stood there, hat in hand, then said, "May I sit down, Ted?"

I hastily waved him into a chair and he seemed relieved to find himself welcome. "A late call?" I said, trying to establish some level of conversation.

"No, just putting something off as long as I could," he said. "Ted, will you loan me the money to go back to her?"

"How much do you need?"

"Four hundred would do nicely."

I started to ask him about his practice but he waved his hand, cutting me off; he didn't want to talk about anything and I understood how much it had really cost him to come to me this way. I got a key and unlocked a cash box I kept in my bottom desk drawer and counted out the money.

He got up, pocketed it, then said, "I was hoping I could count on you, Ted."

"Why, Walter, you—"

He shook his head, turned to the door and walked out.

Alfy Hulse told me later that Walter Ivy remained sober that night and took the morning train.

—18

Two events of great importance to me happened in the summer of 1876: Angeline Hulse gave birth to a boy and he was named Harry Calender Hulse; I promptly dispatched a telegram to Harry in Cincinnati, knowing he would be immensely pleased and flattered.

On July 2nd, Christina went to the hospital and I paced up and down the hallway and decided then and there that every hospital ought to have a rubber room for prospective fathers. Dr. Strudley was the attending physician and Mrs. Murdock was really snapping orders to the nurses, and in due time, with no complications at all, I became the father of a girl, which was what I wanted all the time anyway.

And before you think that doctors get this attention for nothing, let me put in that I promptly paid the bill, a hundred and thirty-one dollars and took my wife and infant home three days later.

I hired a maid, a girl from Goliad who was half Spanish, half French, and had an addition built onto the back of the house to accommodate her. She was quite young, hardly more than a child, and each month she sent ten dollars to her mother because there were two younger sisters to support and no steady work except washings and the like.

Unfortunate people are really unfortunate.

That summer brought great news for Colonel Ranald MacKenzie had moved all the Comanche and Kiowa Indians to a large reservation just north of the Red River in the Indian Nations, and Texas knew what it was to live for once without hostile threat.

Walter Ivy never wrote to me at all through the preceding winter and that summer and I wondered what he was doing, and how he was doing, and whether or not he had patched things up with Dorsey; a man can worry about things like that.

But I couldn't worry long because my position in the community had expanded with the population growth and the hospital required most of my attention and I was very happy with my wife and baby daughter, so I really didn't care what Walter J. Ivy was doing.

This may sound a bit heartless, considering what I owed Walter Ivy, but I lived in Texas, which was big and robust and growing like untended weeds, and of course it was Texas, the land of the paradox and the extremes. Towns like Victoria, with robust leadership, were sporting cement and brick sidewalks and afternoon tea for the ladies was a popular thing and every parent of any means made sure their daughter finished high school and the son went on to college. We had our churches and our community theater and our hospitals and all the culture we could get or afford, and a lot we really couldn't afford.

Still Texas was the frontier, wild, with wild men and wild cattle and a man might wear a waistcoat and hard hat in town, but when he passed beyond the limits he wore a pair of .44 pistols and knew how to use them or he might not reach his destination.

Texas railroads were laying down new rails, but the stagecoach was still the way to travel if you wanted to hit any but the bigger cities. Farmers came in by the hundreds and settled and really it didn't change the complexion of the country much; Texas was cattle, with vast empires ruled by stern barons.

I really had no time to worry about Walter Ivy. Rather I put my faith in human nature, and knowing Walter Ivy's restless spirit, I rather looked for him to come back.

He would find Texas changed. We had law, grand juries, county attorneys, judges, small claims courts, and the largest outlaw and cattle rustler population in the entire west. And for boyhood heroes, Texas youth had the notorious Judge Roy Bean, John Wesley Hardin, and other popular gunfighters.

Doctors no longer pulled teeth as a sideline; we had bona-fide dentists with degrees of such solid character that they no longer had to travel about in a wagon to escape the wrath of outraged patients.

We even organized a county medical society, of which I was elected secretary and treasurer, and it pleased me to have Dr. Strudley serve as the first president. We were a proud and dedicated part of the state medical society and now it was not possible for some half-trained charlatan to set up practice and bilk sick people with candy pills and snake oil.

The society examined credentials most carefully and any doctor wishing to practice had to be a member of the local society, or he just didn't get anywhere at all.

Monopolistic it may be, but we were protecting the health of our patients, and to each of us this was of the highest importance.

And Walter Ivy came back on Christmas Eve.

Christina and I were holding an open house; perhaps twenty people cluttered our parlor with laughter and talk and I was having such a good time that I didn't even hear anyone knock. Then I saw our housekeeper motion to me and I went up to her. "There's a gentleman here to see you, Doctor."

Oh Lord, I thought, not a patient tonight. I went with her to the entrance foyer and she opened the door. Walter Ivy said, "If this is a bad time, Ted, I can come back."

"Well for gosh sake! Come on in, Walter." I started to take his arm then I saw someone standing down on the walk and I leaned forward to see and when I couldn't I switched on the porch light. "Dorsey!" I went to meet her; she had a child in each arm and I put my arm around her and led her to the porch. "What are you standing out here for? Go on in, Walter. René, fetch Mrs. Bodry." I was simply bubbling with words.

Dorsey said, "Ted, please, can we go to your study? I don't want to—well, to meet anyone just yet."

"Certainly," I said and went ahead and opened the door. When they stepped in I snapped on the light and closed the door. "Put the baby on the sofa there. Say, that's a husky looking boy." I took the oldest from her and he promptly grabbed my nose and pulled. Strong little devil.

I put the boy on the floor and he crawled about.

"Sit down," I said. "When did you get in, Walter?"

He looked at his watch. "Eighteen minutes ago. The hotel was full-up. Damned unusual, isn't it?"

"Being the junction of the railroad brings a lot of travelers to town. I hope you've come back to stay."

I tried not to pointedly stare or to appear to be examining them, but it was difficult not to. Walter's suit was showing wear and Dorsey was not dressed in the fashionable way she always liked.

Walter seemed a bit nervous and kept running his hands through his thin hair and Dorsey made an elaborate study of her fingernails. Then he said, "I'd like to find a situation here, Ted. But I suppose now there isn't much for a man in private practice."

Christina knocked on the door and I stepped out into the hall quickly. "Will you give us a few minutes, honey?" I spoke softly.

"Is something the matter?"

"I'm not sure. All right?"

She kissed me lightly. "Sure, Ted."

Then I went back in; Walter and Dorsey had been whispering and they broke it off quickly. "Would you like a drink? The jolly season, you know."

Walter shook his head. "I'm on the wagon, Ted.

210

You might as well know it straight; I hit bottom. Lost a patient. There was a suit. Took everything I had. Everything Dorsey's parents left her. You're looking at a man who got here on borrowed money, Ted." Then he gave a humorless laugh. "I left here that way too, didn't I?"

"Hell, that doesn't matter, Walter. Dorsey, can't I get you something?" She looked at me as though I had offered her charity, but she said nothing, just shook her head.

I sat down and looked at them. "What made you decide to come back here, Walter?"

"Where else could I go?"

It was a good question.

Dorsey stopped toying with her fingers and looked at me. "I know you don't have a very high opinion of me, Ted."

"I did until you taught me different," I said. This was no time to be subtle or polite.

"If I'd have stuck with Walter perhaps none of this would have happened; isn't that what you think?"

"I wouldn't care to speculate on that, Dorsey. But you made Walter reach for something he didn't want and stretch too far to get it. You can't tear a man apart, Dorsey, and expect him to come to much." I looked at Walter Ivy. "Did they revoke your license to practice?"

"No," he said. "There just wasn't any practice. Patients simply switched to another doctor." He shifted his feet. "When I left here, I didn't have much of a practice. I guess I drank it away."

"You guess?"

"All right, I drank too much. But that's over now. I want to get started again. Small, of course. I have no equipment now. And no money."

"Well, I can ask the county medical board to meet after Christmas," I said. "It's their decision."

He looked at me steadily for a moment. "So you have that out here too now, huh? Who's the president? You?"

"No. Archibald Strudley."

Walter laughed again. "Hell, I might as well forget it."

"You're not giving the man any credit at all," I said. "He's not narrow-minded, Walter. Let the board convene. I can offer you a position at the hospital. It'll be salaried, but you can get along on it and in time build up enough savings to start again."

"How much time?" Dorsey asked.

I shrugged. "Depends on how much you can save."

"You're not answering my question," Dorsey said in that hard tone she could fetch up on a moment's notice.

"All right, Dorsey, the salary is forty dollars a week and office space. Walter will be my assistant. He will see the patients referred to him and that's all. He'll also be admitted to membership in the county medical society and in two or three years, when they find out he's not back on the bottle, he can go into private practice. Now that is the best I can do, Dorsey. It'll mean living in a small house and washing your own clothes, but there's nothing disgraceful in that."

I expected her to suck in her breath and go into an outraged tantrum, but she simply said, "Ted, I think that's generous. Don't you, Walter?"

"Yes, more than I'd hoped for."

"Now won't you please come and join the party?" I said. "René can bed the children down in the nursery and you can have the bedroom in the east wing for yourselves. Please accept it as something willingly offered."

"You're very kind, Ted. And thank you," Dorsey said.

I called René and Christina came in and Dorsey took the two children and went out with them.

After the door closed, Walter Ivy said, "They'll have a good cry. I wish to hell I could, Ted. It might make me feel better." He sighed and patted his pockets, but he was out of cigars and I offered him one of mine, and over his protest, shoved four more in his pockets. "Sixty thousand dollars, Ted, that's what it cost Dorsey. And I don't understand it. Not to this minute I don't."

"Don't understand what, Walter?"

"Why she did it. Took her money and bailed me out." He sighed and hid behind a wreath of cigar smoke. "I didn't know her parents had died, Ted. She was unbelievably angry at me for leaving her like I did. When I went back she wouldn't let me in the house. So I stayed at a men's club. Then my trouble came and it was a pretty lonely feeling, no wife, no one to turn to." He sighed. "It was what they're now calling appendicitis in some circles, but it's still perityphitis to me. She was a lovely girl, twelve years old with ringlets two foot long down her back. The attack came on suddenly and I prescribed a strong cathartic. She was dead in eleven hours and the autopsy showed pus throughout the abdominal cavity."

"Dreadful, Walter. But hardly grounds for a suit."

He smiled and shook his head. "When her father came to see me, I was drunk. The child's nurse also said that I smelled like a hot mince pie. The father was wealthy, a man of influence. It never got to court, of course. Dorsey heard about it and it was settled quietly in chambers."

"You didn't send for her?"

Walter shook his head. "No, she came to me. She paid the attorney in cash. Sold the house, everything, to do it. Then she looked at me and said, 'Well, Walter, we do have to go on living, don't we?' I haven't figured out what she meant by that. We talked. I knew it was impossible for me to continue any kind of practice, and we had to live. She had no home. I had none. A friend

214

with a good deal of pity loaned me train fare for the four of us and forty dollars. I've got eleven left."

"I wish I could offer you more, Walter. Believe me."

"I'm glad to get this," he said. "It's more than I expected." He smiled. "I'd have been a poor risk for a loan but I'd have asked for one. The pride's gone, Ted. Dorsey's too, I'm afraid. And I'm sorry about it."

"Why?"

"Well, she's a proud woman."

"Too proud."

He shrugged. "I won't argue it. But it'll hurt me to see her wash clothes and scrub floors."

"It won't hurt her. It'll do her a lot of good, Walter."

"Well, you always were the optimistic one, Ted. She's a good woman, Ted. Stubborn, vain, and proud like you say, but I love her. God knows where I'd be today without her. It'll take a lifetime to pay her back."

"Don't do it."

He frowned. "But it was her money, Ted. All she had in the world. Her inheritance."

"Damn it, Walter, it was the only thing she ever gave to the marriage. Don't be an ass and take that away from her. Fact is, I think it might be the only thing she ever gave anyone. She did it because she loves you. Be thankful for that."

"I hope you're right."

"Walter, I feel sure I am. Live now. No fancy servants to wait on her. Let her be a woman. She may turn out better than you thought." Then I got up and took his arm. "Now come and join the party; I insist."

"This will be embarrassing for me, Ted."

"So what? What do you expect to do, pull a sack over your head and go around that way so no one will know you?" I opened the door and propelled him into the hall. Then we went in to join the others.

—19

The meeting of the county medical board was in the supervisor's board room at the courthouse, and to facilitate business—and because our membership was small—these meetings were always jointly held with the societies of the neighboring counties.

On calling the roll, I found that representatives from the counties of Calhoun, Refugio, Goliad, Lavaca, and Jackson were there, as well as our own county, Victoria.

The agenda was quite long, but finally we got down to that singular item, membership, and Walter J. Ivy's name was offered. There was no immediate objection and I didn't think there would be, but the matter was open to discussion, and Dr. McCaffe, who had friends in the east and kept in touch, had something to say.

Everyone had something to say, and I would like to be able to claim that it was my brilliant argument that saved Walter Ivy's application, but it didn't turn out that way. Reason being that Dr. Strudley wished to debate the matter with Dr. McCaffe, and in order to legally do so he appointed me chairman pro-tem for the duration of the motion and I had to sit there and keep my mouth shut.

In the final analysis it was agreed that each of us was a good deal less than perfect and that each of us could clearly remember standing by and watching a patient die because we had been stupid, or ignorant, or smug enough to make a hasty diagnosis and find it wrong. Walter Ivy had been unfortunate in that the patient's parents were in a position to destroy him, but his misfortune was not a lifetime condemnation, and his application would receive a favorable vote from the society.

So Walter Ivy became an employee of the hospital, the doctor who was always there, on call throughout each day and all night two nights a week. It must have been humiliating for him, to have no patients of his own, and to be subject to the orders of every doctor in the place.

The most familiar sound in the hospital became, "Dr. Ivy, would you assist me, please?"

Within ten days I found a house that Walter could rent; it was a small place, just four rooms with a nice yard and a garden and Christina and I had mixed emotions when they left our house. We didn't want to see them go yet we were delirious with joy that they were going, for Dorsey had to work very hard to keep from being snappy and resentful.

She had made her decision, her bargain, yet she wasn't quite reconciled to living with it. It would take time and I'd just as soon she did it on her own, and in her own house.

The first day of 1877 was clear and cold and there was a rime of ice on the water bucket on the back porch when I woke and carried in wood for the kitchen stove. After breakfast I walked to the hospital and Mrs. Murdock was waiting with a report; every morning she did this, bringing me up to date on what had transpired during the night. We always had a dozen railroad men in the hospital; it seemed to be an average that did not vary much one way or the other, and as soon as one was discharged, another would be brought in.

I spent the morning checking records and hospital business, then I heard the whistle at the roundhouse and started to take out my watch, thinking that it couldn't be noon already. But the whistle kept blowing, short, strident blasts.

"Wreck!" I said to the empty room.

As I came out of my office, Mrs. Murdock hurried down the hall, a roster in her hand.

"Dr. Ellsworth and Dr. McCaffe are here. Dr. O'Brien and Dr. Ivy are on the second floor wards. Shall I summon them, Doctor?"

"Yes, in my office. Tell them not to rush; it makes the patients apprehensive. Where is Dr. Strudley?"

"At home, sir. It's his day off."

"Have someone go for him."

I stepped back into the office and turned to the window that gave me a good view of the town and the main street. As I watched, a minute went by, then another, and then I saw the man running toward the hospital, mackinaw flapping, legs pumping.

He stormed in, panting, and I made him sit down and poured him a drink of whiskey, not that he needed it, but it would calm him. "Doc, some bandits blew the trestle on San Fernandez Creek south of Gussettville! They thought it was the payroll train, but it wasn't. It was the work train goin' to end of track!" He looked at the bottle. "Could I have another hook of that?" I poured and he downed it.

"It's bad then," I said. "How many were hurt?"

He shook his head. "The conductor shinnied up

a pole, cut in to the telegraph wires and called back. The train's derailed. It's real bad, Doc." He wiped his mouth. "There's a train leaving in fifteen minutes. Murray McCloud will hold it that long for you."

"You tell him that will be fine."

When I stepped out, Mrs. Murdock and the others were waiting in the hallway. I said, "Dr. Ellsworth, you're to remain here with Dr. Strudley when he arrives. The rest of you bring bandages, morphine, all the supplies you can carry. Mrs. Murdock, have Guy Hulse bring up litters, blankets and all that and load a wagon; we'll meet him at the train."

"Right away, Doctor." She moved on down the hall.

"I'll meet you gentlemen at the train. Be quick and dress warmly; we may be out there all night and then some."

I gathered what I thought I would need, bundled in my heavy coat, put on overshoes and made sure that I had mittens and a wool scarf. Then I went to the railroad yard and Murray McCloud's office; it was a madhouse and he was barking rapid-fire orders. When he saw me he waved me inside and in a moment came in and closed the door.

"Goddamned bandits," he said. "Mexicans, the way I got it. There were a hundred men on that damned train, Ted. God knows how many of 'em are dead or crippled." He flapped his arms wildly. "The whole train went off, engine to caboose. The engine's in the creek. The boiler blew up. Scalded the engineer and fireman to death. Oh, Jesus, you don't know how a railroad man hates this!" He looked out the window where the work train was making up, a huge crane looked like a gigantic, gaunt bird, all neck and no beak. A string of caboose cars was being hooked up. Then he turned back to me. "The dispatcher has cleared the track and we'll keep it clear, because we're going to highball, Doc." He turned again to the window. "Say, ain't that your man with a wagon?" He flung open the window and yelled down. "Hulse! Hey, Hulse! Take that over to the caboose where the rest of the stuff's being loaded!" Then he waved and slammed the window shut, closing out the inrush of cold air. Then he poured a drink for himself. "Someone coming with you?"

I nodded and he seemed relieved. "Murray, when we start to bring the injured back, I'll want two of your caboose cars. We'll spray the insides thoroughly with antiseptics and—"

"Christ, you can paint them sky-blue-pink for all I care. The railroad's yours, Doc." He grabbed up his mittens and buttoned his coat. "It's time to go. I hope you told your wife you wouldn't be home for supper."

"Mrs. Murdock will take care of that," I said. "She takes care of all the details."

"Yeah," McCloud said. "You ever want to get shed of that wonderful old bitch, I'll make her division super. If I didn't have a wife and four kids I'd marry her myself. They just don't make 'em like that any more."

We left the building and walked across the confusing mass of the switch yard; everyone ran around, yelling orders and it was amazing to me that anything was done, but it was, quickly, and correctly. The train was made up, two engines hooked in tandem, huffing and breathing as though they just couldn't wait to let all out and get rolling.

Walter Ivy and the others were there, on the rear platform of the caboose. Guy Hulse had his wagon parked nearby; it had been unloaded.

I called out to him: "Guy, have the ambulance waiting when we get back. See if you can get the undertaker's hearse and any other carriage that's closed."

"How about Herman Muller's meat wagon?" he yelled.

The train lurched forward and I bobbed my head and he waved and turned the team around. With two engines pulling, the train picked up speed rapidly and it rocked along and the clack of the trucks over the rail joints picked up in tempo.

The pot-bellied stove was kicking out heat and McCloud passed coffee all around. "It's two hundred miles to the wreck," he said, glancing at his big railroad watch. "The engineer tells me he can hit seventy-five most of the way and eighty after he passes the Gussettville siding. That puts us about three hours out."

Linus McCaffe looked around nervously. "Seventy-five, by God that's pretty fast, ain't it?" He tried to sound as though he reached this velocity as a common occurrence, but he was thinking what we were all thinking, that that was a fair clip, and a little faster than we liked to go.

There wasn't much talk; we drank coffee and smoked and Murray McCloud took out his watch quite often and then he said, "Seventy-eight point three miles an hour. Old Ernie must have the throttle bent."

Dr. O'Brien said, "How can you tell?"

"Count the telegraph poles," McCloud said. "I know how far apart they are and I look at my watch. The rest is simple arithmetic."

"I wish you hadn't told me," John O'Brien said.

We slowed through Goliad and Aransas, to about fifty, and then built up speed again. And after slowing briefly for the Gussettville siding the engineers really opened it up.

We slowed finally and arrived at the scene of the wreck at two-thirty in the afternoon and all I can say is, thank God it wasn't night. Of course the trestle went up along with a case of dynamite and the engine and tender were flung up and over, landing upside down in the creek bed, where the engine's boiler exploded. The rest of the cars, about six flat cars and ten work cars, ran on over the horrible wreckage, spilling and tumbling and breaking and flinging themselves every which way.

The survivors—and there were at least forty men moving around—had organized into work crews, aided by a work train that had come out of the Gussettville siding and had gone back before we arrived. There must have been seventy-five men in the Gussettville crew and most of them were working furiously, laying down a temporary siding; the ties were in and the rails were being laid.

But understand that in dealing with such heavy equipment, nothing is done quickly; it all takes time, hours of time. Our concern was for the injured, and there were so many that it was difficult to know where to start.

Right away I had the last caboose unloaded; this would be pushed onto the siding as soon as the switch was put into the main line, and in the meantime I had Dr. McCaffe set up a first aid station in the car to take care of the walking wounded and those only slightly hurt. In this category I placed broken arms and cracked ribs.

It is not possible to describe with words the sounds of such an accident. We arrived roughly four hours after it had happened and still there were men buried in the wreckage, men alive and screaming for help, or for someone to kill them and end their agony.

Blankets were used to wrap the living as they were gotten out. The dead—some of them anyway—were being moved to one side and laid on the bare ground. I counted sixteen and guessed that that number would double before we were through.

I told Dr. O'Brien to stay with one crew that was digging into a jungle of sheared lumber and bent steel, and Walter Ivy went with another.

Toward evening a company of Texas Rangers arrived; they reported briefly to McCloud that the Mexican bandits had been stopped before they reached the border and they were on their way now to a place north of Rio Grande City where the Mexicans were holed-up and making a fight of it.

As the mangled and maimed were being removed and our morphine supply dwindled, I made a decision. I found McCloud and drew him to one side. "Murray, I've got eight men, very bad. I suppose there's another twenty or thirty in there somewhere, alive. But I can't wait. If I do, some of these men will surely die. I've got four certain amputations, one both legs above the knee. I can't get enough morphine into them to kill the pain without killing them."

"Do you want to send the train back now?"

"That's six hours before it'll get back," I said. "That's too long, Murray. It's a case of waiting and having some of these men die or sending the train now and surely having others die." I scrubbed a hand across my mouth. "You have two engines. Can you get everything except one engine and a caboose on the siding?"

"Yes. Touchy, but it can be done."

"And can you get a man up the pole to cut into that telegraph line?"

"No trouble."

"Then what I want to do is put the worst cases in the caboose. I'll write out a wire to Dr. Halverson in Gussettville. He can do his best, which will be far better than we can do here now, and when we take the rest back we can stop and pick them up and then go on to Victoria and the hospital."

"Sounds good," Murray said. "Give me twenty minutes." He dashed off, yelling orders and I sat down and took a leaf from my notebook and composed a message.

Dr. Elmer Halverson
Gussettville,, Texas

Placing in your care these desperately injured. No facilities here for operative measures. Do your best and accept my apologies for placing in your hands an impossible situation. However, it is much worse here. If possible, prepare patients to be moved when hospital train comes through late tonight or early morning.

Regards,
T. Bodry, M.D.

The work train was slowly backing; it had left one engine idle on the main line near the wreck and the rest of the train backed far down the track and there dropped off a caboose, then inched forward on the hastily laid siding. I could see it settle as the weight of the crane car moved onto it and there was a great deal of creaking as the rails took the weight. And as soon as the last car had cleared the switch and it could be thrown, the engine idling on the main line backed up, connected to the caboose and pulled forward again.

The injured were loaded and I sent Dr. McCaffe back with them; he would return as soon as possible. McCaffe's complexion was gray as I gave him instructions: "Remain with Dr. Halverson and assist him in any way. You'll likely be in surgery for two hours. Give him any supplies he needs, then return with the train."

He kept nodding his head and looking at me. "God," he said, "it's awful, isn't it?"

"I imagine it's like war," I said. "Good luck.

Save who you can and don't weep for those you lose."

"I think I will anyway," he said and I jumped down as the train started to move backward, picking up speed.

——20

It was amazing how Murray McCloud could maneuver the train, sorting out what he wanted; I thought it was like a serious game of checkers on wheels, a series of clever moves that reversed the order of the engine and wrecking crane so that it could be backed up to the wreck and lift rubble and debris out of the tangle.

When night fell, lanterns were rigged on poles, and two men carried a wooden case of ammunition clear of the wreck scene and fired star shells into the air where they burst and cast a bright, unearthly light over the whole landscape. This was not continuous, only when someone wanted a moment of clear light to fasten a clevis, or when we were trying to bring a man out.

Some cowboys came to the wreck just before midnight and they had a chuck wagon and a large canvas tent and a huge cast iron stove that took eight men to unload. I later realized that this had come out of the ranch house when I saw the wall collar still on the pipe, a brightly painted circle of tin to match someone's wall paper.

They built a huge bonfire and lit the stove and cooked a meal, beef, potatoes, some string beans, and about fifteen apple pies. The coffee was made in twenty gallon pots, cowboy coffee, strong enough to float a horseshoe, and scalding hot.

It was the best food I ever tasted.

The cook made a large cauldron of soup for the injured men; hot soup or broth can give strength to a sick man better than a pound of beef steak. Murray McCloud had some of his men ladle it out and feed it to the injured.

Of all of us, Walter Ivy was more qualified here because of his military and wartime experiences. We all were shocked, stunned by the enormity of the wreck and the number of injured, but Walter had seen it before, not here, but he had seen it, dealt with it, and was less disturbed by it.

Around three o'clock in the morning we got all those out who were still alive and Murray McCloud had the train on the main line, ready to roll. One of his men was atop the pole with his emergency key and when he shouted down the all clear the conductor waved his lantern and we started back.

Twenty-one dead men on a flat car and the two caboose cars jammed with badly wounded. The other men, most of them bandaged or broken somewhere, rode in another car.

Dr. O'Brien looked completely exhausted; we all were, red-eyed and dog tired. We drank coffee and smoked cigars; McCloud's cigars because we had given all of ours away. Finally O'Brien said, "I wonder how Linus made out in Gussettville?"

McCloud looked at his watch again. "You'll know in forty minutes, Doc."

"Maybe I don't really want to know," O'Brien said. "What a mess. How long will it take you to clear that out of there, McCloud?"

"Three days. We'll work around the clock on it." He yawned and rubbed his eyes. "Hell of a way to start the new year, isn't it?"

"It's a hell of a way any time," Walter Ivy said.

We smoked our cigars awhile, then I said, "Walter, you've been to war. Does a man ever get used to seeing a thing like this?"

"Never," he said flatly. "If he does, he's no good to anyone." He took his cigar out of his mouth and looked at it. "Ted, a doctor has to be clinical as hell because he sees a lot of suffering and more than his share of dying, and he can't go to pieces over it. But in the privacy of his own soul he can cry over it. No, a doctor must be clinical all right, but he must also be the kind of a man who is so outraged by death that he will not rest until a cure has been found or a technique developed to arrest that which offends him." Then he looked up at each of us, seemingly embarrassed because he had made a speech.

John O'Brien butted out his cigar and said, "Dr. Ivy, I want you to know that I'm very happy to have you on the hospital staff."

"Why—thank you," Walter said and looked at the scuffed floor of the caboose.

The train finally reached Gussettville and I went to the vestibule and leaned out as it slowed for the station. There was a large crowd and many lanterns and Dr. Halverson was there, and McCaffe; they had six of the men in a large wagon, bundled in blankets and these men were gently lifted into one of the cars.

Halverson and I met on the platform; he was a man in his forties, and a bit grim about the mouth now. He shook his head and said, "I couldn't save two, Doctor. I'm sorry. Terribly sorry." He was very depressed about it.

McCaffe had been tending the loading and he came up, blowing on his hands. He shook Halverson's hand. "It was an honor to assist you, Doctor. I took the liberty of making a list of the supplies we used. I'm sure Dr. Bodry will have them replaced on the next southbound." He looked at me. "I'd better get aboard." He clapped Halverson on the shoulder and left us.

"Would you be so kind as to send me your report and bill?" I asked. Then I took his arm firmly. "Doctor, I have three cars of injured men there. How many of them do you think are going to die before I can get them into surgery? Now go home and drink some whiskey and get some sleep. And accept my everlasting thanks for your work tonight."

The conductor was signaling and I hopped aboard as the train started to move. The engineer had the all clear and he bent the throttle again, but I was getting used to it, or beyond caring.

We arrived in Victoria just as dawn was breaking and Guy Hulse had the ambulance there and the hearse and several other wagons, including the meat wagon and the grocer's delivery van. I went on ahead to the hospital and Mrs. Murdock was waiting.

"Dr. Ellsworth and Dr. Strudley slept the night here," she said. "We've set up all the spare beds; everything is ready."

"Mrs. Murdock, we'll have them in the offices before we're through; there's that many."

She didn't turn a hair. "Doctor, we're ready for that too. Your wife is coming over and I've put on ten suitable women from town to assist in the nursing. Over your authority, I've cancelled all time off for the next forty-eight hours."

I shocked her immeasurably by kissing her cheek and saying, "You're a jewel."

"Oh, my!" She turned and scurried down the hall and that was the only time I ever saw her flustered.

Then the ambulances began to arrive and the gurneys ran up and down the hall and Mrs.

Murdock supervised the whole thing like a foreman directing steers into the night pens. All surgery cases—and there were nineteen—went on the main floor where Dr. Ellsworth and Strudley examined them, taking the most desperate first. I joined them, scrubbed up and left the rest to Mrs. Murdock.

Seven amputations in a row; it was like a sterile slaughter yard. We were all slightly nauseous from the anesthetic but we could not stop. Dr. Ellsworth's gown became so sodden with blood that he finally tore it off and threw it in the corner and continued to operate in the top of his underwear.

I was conscious of people coming and going, of people helping me. Once I looked up and saw Christina assisting, and another time, at the head of the table, Dorsey. Was that Dorsey?

Seven amputations, and two men died on the table and they were taken quickly out. There was a crushed chest; we couldn't save him, and there were successions of horrible wounds caused by shredded timbers and splinters and steel.

Two nurses scrubbed the floor constantly and Dorsey got down on her hands and knees, like a man searching for a lost collar button and sponged and wiped the floor beneath our feet so we would not slip.

At a quarter after twelve there were no more patients being wheeled through the swinging door and we looked at each other as though we couldn't believe it. It was a nightmare finally closing and we stumbled out and into the hallway. Strudley, the indomitable Englishman, was looking a little peaked and trying not to hide it. We went through the back entrance and let the cold, fresh air clear our heads.

No one said anything. There wasn't anything to say. Ellsworth, always a good surgeon, had risen to new heights, overcoming fatigue and nausea. He had made no mistakes. If the man could be saved, he was saved on that table and we all knew it.

Mrs. Murdock came out and took me by the arm. "Come along now, Doctor. We'll clean up and then I have a nice pill for you so you'll get some rest. Come along like a good boy now?"

We went to my office; it was the only one not crowded with cots and she made me wash up and stretch out on the leather couch. There she was, glass of water in one hand and a pill in the other. Too tired to argue I took it, stretched out and remembered her smiling as she closed the door.

When I woke it was dark outside, but the light over my desk was on and I groggily sat up and looked at my watch.

Twelve-thirty.

She had ears like a cat and I must have made some noise; she was in the room with her stern face and spotless uniform. I said, "Mrs. Murdock, how many times a day do you change your uniform?"

"Six," she said dryly.

"And what do you do in your spare time?"

"Laundry," she said. "How are you feeling, Doctor?"

"Like a mule kicked me. And the others?"

"They've all had some rest. We play no favorites around here, Doctor."

I laughed. "Mrs Murdock, you're the kindest, most considerate woman I've ever known." Then I looked at her steadily. "And I would venture to say that your husband knew what a jewel he had."

"Adelbert and I were very happy," she said, her eyes suddenly smiling. "When he died, my grief was tempered by the knowledge that I was one of the few women who had ever known complete fulfillment." Then she turned starchy and proper again. "If you'd like, Doctor, I'll fix you a cup of tea."

"Thank you, Mrs. Murdock. I'd like a cup. You might bring a pot and invite any of the others in. We might as well get on with the grisly business of statistics."

"I've already done that, Doctor."

She went out and I sat down behind my desk and rubbed my hands over my face. I needed a shave badly, but that could come later. Tomorrow or the next day.

Aaron Stiles from the newspaper came in a few

235

moments before Dr. McCaffe and O'Brien arrived. Then Walter Ivy came in with Dr. Strudley, who said, "Dr. Ellsworth is sleeping."

"Let the poor man have his rest," I said and waved them into chairs. "Gentlemen, you all know Mr. Stiles. He's looking for something to print." I glanced at Archibald Strudley. "How bad is it?"

"Well, of the total train crew, there are twenty-one dead, thirty-two with minor injuries, and fifteen on the critical list. We lost four here and Dr. Halverson lost two." He sighed. "It sounds appalling when you call them out like that, in numbers, but considering the seriousness—yes, the hopelessness of those six men, we've done a job of it. A bully good job."

I looked at the others. "Would any of you care to add to that?"

O'Brien shook his head; so did McCaffe.

"We'd have lost double that five years ago," Walter Ivy said softly. "And how many would be dead now if we didn't have this hospital?"

No one wanted to speculate, but they knew what he meant.

Without saying anything about it, I knew that we would all be on round the clock duty; I didn't thank them because they didn't expect it and wouldn't have wanted it.

The meeting was concluded and they left, except Walter Ivy and Aaron Stiles. He folded his notebook and turned to the door. "It was a bad thing all right. A real bad thing."

Then he went out and from the window I saw him hurry up the street.

Mrs. Murdock came in. "Two nurses would like to see you, Doctor. Of course it's against the rules, but in this case—" She smiled and stepped aside and Christina and Dorsey came in.

Dorsey said, "You look very tired, Walter."

"I've never felt better," he said. "Never." Then he stepped to the window and looked out. A wan sun was shining but the wind husked cold and sharp around the building corner. "When a man finishes twenty-four hours like this he thinks to himself that nothing as bad can ever happen again. But it does, Dorsey. It's trouble. And it's out there, a flood, a typhoon, an earthquake, disease, pestilence; God knows what's really out there. But when it comes, I'm going to be here, Dorsey." He turned and banged his fist down on the desk. "HERE! That's where I'm going to be!"

"I know, Walter," she said softly. "We'll both be here. I'm not afraid." Then she took his arm and turned him to the door. "Why don't you come home and rest? Just for a few hours?"

"Yes," he said. "I'll do that. Will you excuse us, Ted?"

They went out together and I let the silence run; the wall clock ticked loudly and Christina watched me, her eyes warm and full of love.

"And you, Doctor? Where will you be?"

I looked at her and laughed. "Here.

"Walter's going to be all right," I said. Then I sighed and closed my eyes for a moment. "I don't think I'm ever going to catch up on my sleep, Christina."

"Oh, you will. Why don't you come home and I'll fix you some ham and eggs. I don't have to go back on duty for four hours." She came over and put her arm around me. "Humor me, Ted. I'm pregnant again."

What a time to tell a husband! It struck me very funny and I laughed and she watched me, a half smile on her face.

Then she said, "I knew you'd be pleased but I didn't think it was that hilarious." She wasn't angry and I knew it so I got up and put my arms around her and kissed her resoundingly.

Then I put on my coat and we stepped out into the hall; Mrs. Murdock walked up. "I'm going home for a few hours, Mrs. Murdock. If you want me for anything—"

"Everything will be taken care of, Doctor."

"I'm sure it will be," I said, turning toward the entrance. Then I stopped and turned back. "Tell me, Mrs. Murdock, where will you be when the next catastrophe strikes?"

"Why—here, of course. What did you think? This is my home."

Then she turned and stalked off as though she

were going to give the troops a good dressing down. I took Christina's arm and we went out into the biting air. It was a day for walking and I breathed deeply of the flavors carried up from the gulf, a tangy freshness of the sea.

Out of the roundhouse yard a train huffed, loaded with timbers and a full crew, the trestle gang going to rebuild what had a few days before been destroyed. I heard the train whistle for a crossing and then the sound of it was gone, carried away by the wind. Overhead a bird wheeled and tossed, riding the currents, sailing about in great circles.

I stopped and looked at the town, then said, "You know, Christina, a man would be a little crazy if he ever missed any of this."

"Yes," she said, "I know."

Then we walked on to our house.

Center Point Large Print
600 Brooks Road / PO Box 1
Thorndike ME 04986-0001 USA

(207) 568-3717

US & Canada:
1 800 929-9108
www.centerpointlargeprint.com